Twisted
LOCKE

(Locke Brothers, 3)

VICTORIA ASHLEY & JENIKA SNOW

Cover Designer:
Dana Leah, Designs by Dana

Cover model:
Andrew Biernat

Photographer:
Wander Aguiar

Editor:
Kasi Alexander

Interior Design & Formatting by:
Christine Borgford, Type A Formatting

Twisted
LOCKE

Ace

I PLACE THE JOINT BETWEEN my lips and look down to see red covering my knuckles. It gets my adrenaline pumping once again, making me very aware of what happened less than five minutes ago.

My hands are busted up, covered in blood, but I don't feel shit. Nada.

No pain and definitely no motherfucking remorse for almost taking a man's last breath.

This motherfucker should've known better than to cross an angry, homicidal Locke.

It's obvious he was very unaware of who was sitting across the bar from him when he decided to punch his woman in the face and then proceed to grab her by the hair and drag her across the bar as if she was a fucking ragdoll.

The fact that he felt the need, had the fucking balls to do that in a roomful of people, told me he did even worse things to her when no one was around.

He barely made it out the door before I was on his ass, pulling him from her and showing him what it's like to be the fucking ragdoll.

I wanted to make sure he knew what it felt like to be the *helpless* one and I have no doubt he's still feeling it this very moment.

It feels so fucking good to know that some son of a bitch is suffering right this very second, because they chose to make someone weaker than them suffer first.

I'll never get over that feeling . . . the high it brings me to crush a motherfucker even harder than they crushed someone's world.

To leave that permanent scar they deserve.

I'm barely halfway through smoking my joint before I pass it to the woman beside me with the busted-up, swollen face.

"Here. Finish that while I take care of this prick." I slap the trunk and a twisted ass grin crosses my face when I hear a few desperate pounds come from the inside.

He should've thought about his actions. If he had he wouldn't be shoved in some stranger's trunk like a little bitch right now.

Good thing I decided to take the old Dynasty out of the garage tonight.

"Are you going to kill him?" she says, the pain on her face clear as she places the joint between her busted-up lips. She takes a long hit, holding the smoke in.

"Probably not. It depends on him."

My response has the noise coming from the trunk getting louder and more desperate.

"Shut up in there you, fucking asshole!" Her whole body is shaking in anger as she slaps the trunk repeatedly. "Fuck you! I hate you! I fucking *hate* you so much! You're done hurting me. Done! Do you hear me?"

Next thing I know she falls to her knees and bursts into tears.

There's nothing I hate more than seeing a woman hurting and her tears are just enough to set me off again.

"Fucking piece of shit!" I growl out, reaching into the backseat for my hammer.

Before I can even think about what I'm doing, I'm popping the trunk and dragging the sorry motherfucker out by his neck.

"Get up on your hands and knees." I give him a shove in her direction. I help the woman up so she's not kneeling any longer. "In front of her, bastard!" I yell, losing my damn patience. "Now!"

"I'm sorry." He looks up at me, snot covering his pathetic, beat-up face as he does what he's told. "I'm so sorry. I promise I'll never lay a finger on Amanda again. I swear. I fucking swear."

Stepping up behind him, I grab his hair and force him to look straight across so he can get a good view of the damage he did to her. "Look what the fuck you did!" I bend down beside him to make sure he's actually looking. "Do you see the fucking damage you caused?" I slap the back of his head before grabbing his hair again and tilting his head up. "Do you?"

"Yes," he whines. "Yes. I see it."

His woman is backing up and crying so hard now that her whole body is convulsing as she attempts to catch her breath.

"You were damn right when you said you'd never lay a finger on her again. You wanna know why, Frankie?"

He shakes his head back and forth. "No. No. Please!"

"Too motherfucking bad. Place your hands flat on the ground."

Now he's the one shaking.

Good. He should be.

"Now!" I scream and kick him over when he doesn't listen. "Be a man and get this over with, Frankie. Do this for her!" I point my hammer at Amanda, who still looks scared shitless at him being near her.

From the old bruises on her face and arms, it looks as though he's been hurting her for a while now. This shit ends here and now.

"It's either going to be your hands or . . ." I place my hammer to the back of his skull, which has him immediately splaying his hands out on the ground in front of him.

"Fuck, fuck, fuck . . ." he cries to himself, while squeezing his eyes shut. "I'm sorry. I'm sorry . . ."

"Well, I'm not."

Gripping my hammer, I take one hard swing at his right hand, hearing the bones crack as he screams out in pain.

I barely give him a moment to really feel the pain before I take a swing at his left hand, causing him to scream out again before he falls over and begins crying.

Keeping my eyes on him, I reach for a smoke and place it between my lips before bending down beside him. "Just be lucky you're not fucking dead. You'll heal."

He doesn't say anything and from the excruciating pain he's clearly in, I don't expect him to be able to.

I take a few seconds to enjoy my handiwork before I pat his back and walk over to check on Amanda.

She almost looks relieved as she watches him suffer on the ground, as I'm sure she's done plenty of times since she's met this piece of shit.

"I should take him to the emergency room." Her voice is void of any emotion. "He may be hurting for a while."

I honestly don't give a fuck if he writhes in pain on the ground, but Amanda seems worried, and I feel for her. If this will make her feel better, getting this piece of shit to a doctor, then so be it.

"Yeah," I say between drags. "Pull your car up and I'll shove him into the backseat."

She backs up, keeping her eyes on Frankie the whole time. "Yeah . . . okay. I'll be right back."

A black '95 Corvette pulls up a few moments later and I can't help but to laugh to myself. He's going to be real comfortable shoved into the backseat of that thing.

Not my problem and not my damn concern.

"Come on, asshole." I flick my cigarette across the mostly empty parking lot and reach underneath Frankie's arms to lift him to his feet.

Amanda already has the car door open and the seat pushed forward, so I give him a shove toward the car and stuff him into the backseat.

It may seem a little fucking twisted, but I get pleasure from hearing him whine and cry like a little bitch.

I guess that's why I'm the twisted one.

Hurting others brings me pleasure and I'm the first one to admit that I enjoy doing what we do.

It's because of me that my brothers are the way they are. All it took was years of abuse from our sorry ass excuse for parents and seeing the secret lifestyle that our uncle Killian lived.

I did this. I brought my brothers into this lifestyle and twisted is what I do best . . .

Melissa

A TEXT COMES THROUGH FROM Kadence asking me to bring her the leftover scones and muffins when the coffee shop closes for the night.

If we don't take them home, then they just end up getting thrown away, so I send her a quick text to let her know that I'll bring the leftovers home with me.

I'm just about to shove my phone back into my pocket when it vibrates in my hand with another message from my *sometimes* roommate.

Kadence: Bring them to Aston's. I'm already over there.

Kadence: Pleeeeease . . .

I huff and put my phone away without bothering to respond to her message. She's knows I'm still not very comfortable with going to the Locke house, yet it seems she always finds a *reason* for me to show up there.

What she doesn't know, though, is that I'm attracted to the oldest Locke. The most twisted one of them all, the more I see him, the more I'm drawn to him physically.

I've been doing *everything* in my power to make sure I don't fall for a Locke when I've spent the last four years fearing them.

When Kadence fell for the youngest Locke I was against it and wanted nothing more than to keep her away from Aston.

I'll admit I've softened up toward them over time, but I still don't quite understand their violence and that part scares me.

Especially Ace.

He's vicious and mysterious in ways that his brothers aren't, yet when I look at him I feel as if I'll melt into a puddle at his feet.

Ace has this *power* to make me want to fall at my knees with just one glance into his amber eyes.

I've never met a man so dangerously sexy in my entire life and a part of me is unsure if I can stop myself from falling for him if I keep getting sucked into being around him.

Releasing a deep breath, I lean over to clean off a table, but freeze when I glance out the window to see Ace standing across the street, leaning against his truck.

He's got a cigarette between his lips and I can't help but stare at his mouth as he takes a drag from it.

His gaze is trained on the building but I can't tell whether or not he can see me watching him. It has my heart beating at an alarming rate, but I can't seem to pull my gaze from him.

He's dressed in a snug white T-shirt and a pair of black jeans that fit his body to perfection. I hate that he's impossible to turn away from and I hate that he's so physically flawless.

"Too bad a man so incredibly sexy has to have such a bad reputation."

I pull out of my haze at the sound of Gia's voice. I hadn't even noticed she was standing beside me until now.

"It's weird that he's just standing there, staring at the building, right?" I glance beside me to see her staring out the window as she speaks. "He's the oldest one? What's his name . . ."

"Ace," I say on a whisper before she's able to finish thinking. "And yes; he's the oldest one."

A small smile tugs at the edges of Ace's lips before he flicks his cigarette across the street and jumps into his truck.

"I heard that he once cut a guy's finger off and force fed it to him," Gia says, watching as he drives away. "That's some crazy stuff. I can't believe that Kadence dates one of those guys. I'd be terrified."

"They're not that bad," I say on a swallow. "It's not like they go out and just hurt random innocents. They have reasoning behind everything they do."

I'm not sure who I'm trying to convince that the Lockes aren't what they seem, Gia or myself.

The only reason I choose to still be cautious is because I know I *have* to in order to keep Ace at a safe distance.

"Then maybe it's not so bad that the oldest one is hanging around." She smiles and turns away from the window. "Maybe he'll come in next time. I'd love to see that one up close. He's absolutely gorgeous and terrifying at the same time."

The idea that Gia is attracted to Ace for some reason bothers me. It's stupid for me to feel this way.

"Maybe," I say, wiping off the table. "I have a few things to take care of in the back and then I'm going to take off. Do you need help with anything first?"

Gia is the owners' daughter and she's been coming in almost daily for the last few months. I have a feeling it's because she'll be taking over the coffee shop soon so that Cheryl and Bryon can retire.

"No, I don't think so. We'll be lucky to get one, maybe two more customers stopping by so I should be good to handle things."

"Sounds good."

After cleaning up in the back and organizing things for tomorrow, I pack up some leftover pastries and jump into my car, hoping that maybe Ace won't be around when I drop these off to Kadence.

After seeing him already once today, I'm not sure I can handle seeing him for a second time and not end up spending the rest of the night thinking about him.

It's something I've been doing a lot lately and the last thing I need is to keep the habit going.

I need to be strong when it comes to the oldest Locke.

I'm just not sure for how much longer I can manage that . . .

3

Ace

I PLACE A JOINT BETWEEN my lips and watch as the asshole before me struggles to get out of the ropes.

His attempts are only making the rope tighter, digging into his already bloodied wrists even more. I know how to tie a fucking knot, and his struggles only have me grinning. He won't be able to get out of it unless I fucking want him to.

"Take it easy," I finally say and glance down at his wallet, "Troy Foster. You keep pulling at those ropes and you're going to lose your hands."

Hell, keep pulling at those ropes. Give me more entertainment tonight.

He struggles to scream at me, but with the tape wrapped around his mouth, nothing but muffled sounds come out. Tears are coming out of the corner of his eyes, his face is red as a fucking beet, and I can see snot starting to slip out of his nose. The fucker isn't used to this. He wants out, no doubt. He probably wants at me with all that rage. I should just let him go, should just let him get a punch or two in so that I can feel that pain then really go fucking psycho on his ass.

He mumbles something again, his eyes narrowed, the anger coming from him clear.

"What was that?" I kick away from the garage door and walk over to yank his head back. "I couldn't understand you." I push his head down and take a long hit off the joint before yanking his head back again and blowing the smoke in his eyes.

He squints and struggles harder.

"You know . . ." I pull the knife from my boot and run it along his skin as I walk around him. "I'm not sure what to do with you yet. You see . . . I don't like the idea of some stranger coming to my motherfucking house in the middle of the night with a gun."

I stop in front of him and tug on his wrists, which are tied above him. His scream is muffled behind the tape as the ropes dig further into his skin, causing blood to drip down his arms.

"I could *kill* you to make sure that you're never a threat to my family again."

My threat has him struggling against the ropes again, clearly desperate to get away—or maybe to get to me—no matter how much pain he's currently in.

I tilt my head and watch as he shakes his head and attempts to scream.

"Or . . . or I could just chop both your hands off so you can never hold a gun again, never pick a lock, hell," I chuckle, "open a fucking door handle again." I stare at him in the eyes. "I haven't quite decided yet which route I should go, though."

I scowl deeper, letting him know how serious I am. This asshole really has no clue who he's fucked with.

King caught him on the side of the house last night and dragged him down by his foot from the window he was attempting to climb into.

He tore into his leg pretty good before I was able to run outside and see what was going on.

The piece of shit pulled a pistol on me. Aimed that shit right at my head, but King attacked his arm before he could manage to get a shot off.

This asshole fucking almost shot at me. Could've shot at my family and now he's going to pay the price.

Just thinking about it has me wanting to rip his throat out with my bare hands.

With an angry growl, I take my blade and run it down his cheek, watching as the blood drips from the wound.

I'm already covered in his blood as it is, due to the beating I gave him thirty minutes ago after returning from the coffee shop.

I needed something to hold me back from killing this motherfucker tonight, and seeing Melissa always seems to calm the demons inside my head just long enough to get me thinking clearly.

If it weren't for her, he'd already be dead.

Something in me snaps and I find myself taking the blade and running it down his chest, watching as the knife moves easily through his skin, opening up the flesh just superficially, blood welling up immediately.

I'm a sadistic fucker so I make a few more cuts on his chest, the asshole struggling, mumbling behind the tape. His eyes are wild, and sweat is dotting his forehead, mixing with the blood as it runs down his cheek and cut. No doubt that shit stings.

I laugh at that.

I take a step back and stare at my handiwork. He has his fingers clenched tightly, and I see blood on his palms. He relaxes his hands and sags against the bonds, crescent shaped cuts from his nails littering the insides of his hands.

But I'm pissed about him breaking in, about thinking he could threaten me. I'm seeing red, picturing if I'd had Melissa here, how she'd be scared, in danger. I grab one of his hands and start breaking his fingers, snapping the digits back until I hear him screaming, hear the bone splintering in two. Only then do I exhale roughly and move away.

"We're done for tonight, Troy." I take one last hit from the joint and toss it at his face, embers bouncing against his skin. "Expect me when the sun rises. I have a few games I want to play with you tomorrow."

Tears run down his face and I grin, but other than the pleasure I feel at exacting pain in him, I don't feel shit for this sorry fucker. He didn't give a fuck when we came here with the intent to hurt whoever was inside, to take what wasn't his.

He wasn't sorry when he aimed that pistol at my head and tried to take my God damn life.

But he sure as hell is sorry now.

Rolling my head around on my neck, I hear it crack. I step out of the garage and grab a cigarette from my pocket, closing my eyes for a second and just inhaling and exhaling. I open my eyes again and place the cigarette between my lips and look up as headlights come from the driveway.

I stand here and take a drag, needing some kind of release before I lose it on whoever has decided to show up invited.

It's not until the vehicle gets closer that I realize that it's Melissa's car.

Fuck.

This isn't how I wanted her to find me.

She steps out of the vehicle, her gaze immediately landing on me.

From the way her eyes grow wide as she checks out my bare chest, I know without a doubt that she notices the splatters of blood across my skin.

She's heard of the things we do, no doubt. Hell, I know Kadence had probably told her shit that Aston has done with us all in the name of fucking over a Locke. She's even been around after a few jobs, but she's never actually seen me covered in another man's blood before.

I keep my gaze on her, watching intently as she swallows and fights to pull her gaze off me.

I can see the struggle on her face, until she finally manages to turn away and walk to the front door.

Fuck me, she's so damn beautiful that all I want to do is slam her against the side of the house and fuck her right here and now.

I don't even care that I'm covered in another man's blood.

I want to be buried inside her pussy, making her scream for me.

The problem with that . . . Melissa hasn't quite come around to our lifestyle yet.

That's something I plan to change real soon. I've already given her enough time and I'm tired of waiting.

I want her as mine and when I get to her, she's going to want to belong to me just as much as I want her to.

Melissa

I DON'T KNOW WHAT TO think right now. All I can picture is Ace, the blood covering him, his expression feral, his body tense. I picture his cut muscles just under his skin as he stood there, staring at me, maybe wondering what I would do, if I'd run. The light from the garage had silhouetted him, making him seem even more dangerous than he already was.

I haven't been able to get the picture of him covered in blood out of my head. He was standing there looking lethal, as if he could rip a man's heart out with his bare hands and there I was, unable to turn away from him.

What the hell is wrong with me?

I'm so confused with the fact that even knowing he was just

hurting someone, I still found him to be sexy as he stood there staring at me.

I almost hate myself for how aroused I was, how much I wanted him in that moment, even covered by the gore and violence of what he'd just done.

I knew I needed to get away from the Locke house as quickly as possible, before he was able to walk through that door and catch me staring for a third time in one damn day.

After I'd left, Kadence had explained to me what happened with someone trying to break into the house the night before.

It is all so crazy. It seems like an eternity ago that I first met the Locke brothers. I can still remember rooming with Kadence, knowing about them and what they did to anyone who crossed them. They are bad news but I saw the curiosity on Kadence's face and I hated it.

And now here I am just as curious about one of them.

The most lethal and twisted one of them all.

Ace.

Anyone who doesn't know him, anyone who doesn't know of his reputation, his clean-cut appearance would make him seem like the boy next door. But he's far from that. His skin might not be inked like his brothers, but he's even more dangerous than they are.

His hammer is his weapon of choice, and he has no empathy for people who cross him or people who hurt others who are weaker than them. Maybe that's why I'm captivated by him even though I try my hardest not to be.

Maybe that's why I want him so much.

Yes, I'm drawn to a Locke, but I will never admit that to anyone, least of all him. Hell, I try to not even admit it to myself.

But then I see the way he looks at me, the way he touches me, even around his family. He makes me feel owned already and

I haven't even done anything sexual with him. But God, I want to. I want his hands on my body, rough, demanding. I want him to hold me down and take me the way I know he can, with a savage brutality that will make me know there is no one else for me.

I've been feeling this way more and more with each day that passes and I don't know what to do with that. I don't know what the hell is wrong with me.

"Miss?" I snap out of my haze and look at the customer in front of me. She lifts an arched eyebrow and gives me this stiff glare. "I ordered a latte. But you're just standing there."

"Sorry," I mumble and turn away to make her drink. I need to get Ace out of my head, need to worry about working and myself. He might've told me in more ways than one that I was his but a part of me wants to not get involved with a Locke because I know he can be dangerous.

But he's like a drug to me, my addiction that I can't walk away from, can't ignore. I felt that again last night stronger than before and it's been eating at me.

The rest of the day flies by as I try and focus on work. Once I clock out and grab my purse and car keys, my intention is just to go straight home. But as soon as I step out the back door and head to my car, I feel someone watching me. I stop and lift my head to see Ace standing there leaning against his truck, which is parked right beside my car.

The sight of him causes my heart to about leap from my chest. This is the last place I expected to see Ace.

He's got a baseball cap on, a white T-shirt stretched across his muscular chest and arms, and a pair of faded jeans that fit his long, lean body to perfection. His boots are black, slightly scuffed, his legs crossed at the ankles. Shit kickers are what I aptly call them.

He pushes away from his truck and walks over to me. The grin on his face can't be called anything but shit eating. I don't know what to say, or how to act. This is the first time he's ever shown up at my work other than when he was parked out front yesterday.

"Hey," I say and look up at him. He might be lean and muscular like a swimmer, but he's tall and I have to crane my head back just to look at his face. "What are you doing here?" He takes my bag from me and we walk over to my car together. He hasn't said anything yet, but he doesn't have to for me to feel like I'm walking on a tight rope.

"I haven't seen you in a few days and you took off so quickly last night . . ." He looks me right in the eyes and I take my bag from him and toss it in the back of my car.

"I've just been busy with work." I lie easily, my voice tense, stiff. I am trying to not let him see how much he affects me, but I feel I'm failing miserably. I glance at him out of the corner of my eye, see his brows lowered, this look of confusion on his face, or maybe he's pissed. I can't tell half the time with him. He's so hard to read.

The truth is I've been avoiding him. It's not that I don't want to see him, because that's actually the opposite. I want to see him all the time, and that scares me.

What scares me even more is the fact that I still feel this way even after what I witnessed last night.

"You've been busy at work?" He leans against his truck again and crosses his arms. It's obvious that he knows I'm lying.

"I have been." I clear my throat and look away for a second before staring at his face again.

"Let me take you somewhere. Just you and me, a place where we can talk."

I look at his hands, his knuckles, which are scabbed over, and it makes me wonder just what he did to that guy last night. But

I know better than to ask what happened. Because the truth is I don't want to know the answer.

The violent side of Ace, the dangerous part, scares me, even though I know he will never hurt me.

"You want to take me somewhere?"

He nods. "Just you and me."

The thought of being alone with him has my nerves kicking in. I don't want to fall for him. I *can't* fall for him.

When I don't give him an answer, he backs me against my car and closes in on me. His toned arms surround me, and his scent, which I can only describe as intoxicating, fills my head and makes me drunk.

I find myself breathing hard and fast as he presses his body against mine and leans down so that his face is in my hair. I may even be trembling a bit, both out of fear and desire for Ace. "I'm not leaving until you say yes." I feel his lips move against the strands before he lowers his mouth to my ear and lets out something between a growl and a moan. "Fuck, Melissa. You have no idea how hard your scent gets me. But I'm not here to push myself on you and make you realize how much you truly want me inside of you. No . . . I'm here to take you somewhere alone so we can think in some peace and quiet. Now say yes."

His words have my entire being feeling as if it's igniting into flames and the closeness of his hard body has my brain in a mush. I can't think straight when he's so damn close.

"Okay," I say on a tremble. "We can go somewhere alone. But just to relax, to talk." I somehow find the strength to push him away so he's no longer practically glued to me. "And you have to leave your hammer at home. No violence."

He flashes his usual twisted grin that always seems to spark something in me I can't seem to understand. "Done. I left it in the SUV." He reaches out with his scabbed-up knuckled hand and closes my car door. "We'll take my truck."

Oh shit, is the only thing that runs through my mind as I allow him to lead me to the other side of his truck.

What am I getting myself into by allowing the scariest Locke of them all to get me alone?

Ace

IT MAY BE TWISTED TO admit, but feeling the way Melissa's body trembled when I pressed mine against hers fucking turned me on and had my cock jumping with excitement.

I know a part of that is because she somewhat fears me still, but the other part is because she wants me just as much as I want her.

She knows how dangerous I am. She knows I'll kill any motherfucker who threatens my family. But what she doesn't know is that I love just as hard as I intimidate, maybe even more.

I hear a small breath escape her as I grip her waist and hoist her into my truck.

I'm not sure I can ever get used to how damn good it feels whenever I touch her. That's why I need to do everything in my power to make sure she wants me to keep touching her.

Things may get a little ugly, but I'm going to twist her up and shake the fucking innocence in her.

And by the time I'm through with her, she's going to be my beautiful, twisted angel.

When I climb into the vehicle and take off, I can feel her gaze on me as if she's taking this moment to take me all in, most likely thinking that I won't notice since I'm driving.

But fuck me . . . it's hard not to notice.

"Do you like what you see?"

From the corner of my eye, I catch her quickly turn away from me so she's now looking out the passenger side window. "Just checking for any fresh blood or any warning signs that I should jump out of this moving truck and run for my life. Don't get too cocky."

"Is that a deal breaker for you? Because I'm pretty sure you saw me covered in blood last night . . ." I glance over at her and raise a brow. "Yet you're still here in my truck with me."

She's silent after that.

That is, until she notices me pulling onto a side road and into the woods.

"Is this one of your kill spots?"

I laugh. "You're supposed to relax, remember?"

"How am I supposed to be able to relax when the woods are where axe murderers bring their victims before they cut them into tiny pieces and hide their body parts? Or in your case . . ." She turns behind her and begins looking into the backseat. "Smash your victims' body parts until they come off."

"That's not a bad idea. I've never tried that before. It could be a good workout." I park and look over to see her staring at me all wide-eyed and somewhat shocked. "Do you really think I'd do that?"

She watches me as I reach for my cap and take it off before

running a hand through my messy hair. "God, I hope not. I'm not that twisted." I offer her a half smirk and reach over her to open her door. "Come on."

I'm the first one to hop out and I can't help but be a bit amused that she hesitates before getting out herself.

I really have my work cut out with Melissa.

"What are we supposed to do out here in the middle of no-where?"

"Lay back and relax. Talk, shit like that." I flash her a grin. I grab a blanket out of the back of the truck and make my way to the tailgate. I pop the back and lay the blanket down. I jump up before reaching out for her hand. "This is the most peaceful place to think. I've been coming here for years but this will be the first time I've *not* come alone."

"Really?" She finally gives me her hand, allowing me to pull her up beside me. "What do you like to come here and think about?"

I lay back and rest my hands behind my head. "I don't know. Just whatever's going on in my life at the time, I suppose. It's kind of hard to relax and have some *me time* when my brothers are always around and there's always some fucked-up shit for us to handle. This is the one place that is *mine* alone."

She's sitting on the edge, hanging her legs off as she looks up at the sky. "I have to admit that this is a pretty nice spot. I can see why it's so relaxing."

"Come here," I say softly, wanting her to see that I'm not all that bad. I hold my hand out for her to grab. "Lay with me."

It takes her a few seconds, but she eventually takes my hand and allows me to pull her down beside me.

Her gaze locks with mine. I should try to be a gentleman or some shit, but being so close to her has me all in knots, has the possessive side rising up. I crawl above her, spread her thighs with my knees and place my hard body between her legs. I can see her eyes go wide, feel her chest start to rise and fall faster. She breathes harder, and I know that she wants this just as much as I do. "Does this make you nervous?"

I see her throat work as she swallows. After a second she nods. "A little."

I press my body farther between her legs as I lean in to brush my lips against her ear. I know she can feel how hard I am for her. "How about this? Does it make you nervous to *feel* how badly I want you, Angel?"

She nods again. "Yes," she whispers.

"That's all I needed to know."

With that, I roll over and lie back in my spot, allowing her to breathe easily again.

The next hour goes by in silence.

I've got Melissa alone for the first time and although I'd love nothing more than to fuck the fear out of her, to make her see that she is meant to be mine, I hold back because I can tell it's too soon.

I'll take things easy this time, but I can't say the same for the next. My willpower only goes so far.

After a while, she finally sits up and turns to face me. "It's getting kind of late. I should probably get home. Mind taking me back to my car?"

Without saying a word, I sit up and get off the tailgate, grab her hips and pull her closer to me so her legs are hanging off the side, and stare at her. I look into her eyes for a second, wanting to kiss her, to possess her. But I hold back and instead help her down as well.

"Let's go."

Once we get back to her car, I lean across the seat and un-buckle her seatbelt.

I can feel her heavy breaths hitting my neck and I know without a doubt that I've got her walls slowly crumbling.

"Goodnight," she says quickly. "Appreciate the relaxing night. I actually needed it."

I turn my head so that my lips are right above hers as I speak. "Good" is all I say before I lean back to my seat and listen to her uneven breathing.

She'll go to bed thinking about me and that's enough for tonight at least.

It definitely won't be enough for next time . . .

Melissa

I SPENT THE ENTIRE NIGHT tossing and turning, thinking about Ace and how good it felt to be alone with him.

When he first asked me to go somewhere with him I was nervous. I was scared, not sure of what to expect from a guy like him. I never would've imagined that I'd be able to have a *normal* moment with him and enjoy the night as if nothing else mattered.

I'm so damn confused right now, because even though I know he's twisted and dangerous, I also know that there's more to him. There's a side to him that I could easily fall for and get hurt.

Kadence is sure to get a kick out of this and that's why I need to keep my feelings from her until I know exactly what they mean.

"Why did you leave in such a hurry the other night?" Kadence questions from across the diner booth.

"I told you," I say over my glass. "I had a headache and I was tired. Why do you keep questioning my motives?"

She smiles and takes a bite of her cheesecake. It's the whole reason we're here. "It had nothing to do with a shirtless Ace that came inside a few minutes after you left?"

"Why would it? We didn't even talk. I don't know what you're talking about."

She laughs and stands up. "So it had nothing to do with the fact that he looks pretty damn good in red."

"That's messed up." I shake my head and try to fight back the smile. "It was someone else's blood, Kadence. Of course not. I wasn't attracted to him no matter how good he looked."

"So . . . you admit that he looked good?"

"Don't you have to get to work or something? I knew I shouldn't have met you here. I should've known it would lead to me watching you scarf down your cake while you try to get something out of me that will never happen. Ace is . . ."

"The guy you can't stop thinking about." She grins when I give her a dirty look. "Okay. Okay. I'm going. You should get some lunch or something while you're here."

I shake my head. "I'll just finish my drink and eat at home. The cheesecake is on me so leave before I change my mind."

"Thanks, babe." She smiles that annoying smile at me again before finally turning away and walking outside.

I take a moment to finish my drink and pull myself together before I walk out of the diner and to my car.

It's not until I reach for the door handle that I notice Ace's truck parked behind me in the lot.

My stupid heart betrays me at the sight of him and about flies from my chest again. It only gets more intense the more I see him.

I swallow and walk over to his truck at the same time that he hops out and shuts the door behind him.

The way his amber gaze roams over my body makes me hot, and when his gaze stops on my lips, I find myself wondering what it would feel like for Ace to kiss me.

Surely, he'd be rough and demanding.

"What are you doing here, Ace?" I lift a brow and watch as he tosses his keys up and catches them. "Is a Locke brother stalking me?"

His lips pull up into a half smirk that causes my breath to catch in my throat. "You haven't eaten yet. I'm here to buy you lunch."

My heart stops mid-beat as Ace grabs my hand and begins walking us back toward the door of the diner.

A few glances land on us as he opens the door and guides me right back to the table that Kadence and I were just sitting at.

I have to admit that being seen with Ace in public is sort of a rush. I know without a doubt by the surprised looks on everyone's faces that there's not one person in this place that doesn't know that I'm here with a *Locke*.

Ace pushes one of the menus in front of me but doesn't say a word as he grabs for the other menu and begins looking it over.

I find it to be crazy that he can make me feel excited and nervous just by sitting across from me in a diner. He doesn't even have to speak to evoke these emotions inside me.

We both place our order when the waitress comes by a few minutes later. I can tell by the slight shakiness in her voice that Ace makes her nervous, yet she can't stop checking him out and it's driving me crazy.

Just the thought of Ace touching her or kissing her has jealousy rushing through me.

I look across the table to see Ace's attention on me, instead of the waitress who has barely finished taking our order. It's as if he's trying to figure me out.

"Have you ever been in love, Melissa?"

I nod and thank the waitress as she drops off two glasses of water. "Once. What about you, Ace?" He watches me as I take a drink of my water. "Have you ever been in a long-term relationship?"

"No," he says, his gaze locked on mine. "I've been waiting for the right girl to claim as mine. Once I find her . . ." He runs a hand through his messy brown hair before licking his bottom lip to wet it. "She'll be mine for good. That's how us Lockes work."

My heart hammers around in my chest at the idea of belonging to Ace. He wants a girl to possess.

Why do I find that to be so hot?

The food comes a few minutes later and we eat in silence, both of us glancing up to look at the other every few minutes and every time that he does, excitement courses through me.

I can't help but to feel this way and it's driving me insane.

I'm not sure if I'll ever be ready for Ace Locke, yet I can't help but want him . . .

Ace

CALL ME TWISTLKED. CALL ME a fucking stalker and I won't deny that shit. I'll do anything when it comes to getting Melissa.

Melissa looks up when the waitress sets the bill down in front of us, but I decide to keep my attention on her, wanting to show her that I could care less about the hot girl that is checking me out for the tenth damn time since we've walked through the door together.

I'm here for her and her only.

"What are you doing when you leave here?" I ask, tossing down a fifty-dollar bill.

She stands up and reaches into her pocket to pull out some cash. I grab it from her hand and shove it back into her pocket, getting up in her personal space.

Just like before, my closeness has her breathing picking up. This has me lifting her chin up and leaning in close as if to kiss her, but I stop right before our lips can meet. "Are you going to answer me, Angel? Or make me guess."

"Work," she says on a breath. "I have to be at work soon."

I can hear her swallow as I raise my thumb up to brush over her lips. "What about after work?"

"I don't know." She backs away from my touch, but I take a step further, backing her up against the side of the booth. "Probably going home. To bed."

"What if I don't want you to?" I run my hand up the side of her neck, before reaching around to cup the back of it as I lean in close to her mouth again. This has her fighting to catch her breath. "Come for a ride with me tonight. What time do you get off?"

"Ten. Or a little after. It depends."

I release her neck and smile as her gaze lowers to my lips. "I'll be out in the parking lot then."

She nods as I back away, giving her room to walk around me.

I know I'm not exactly *easy* to fall for, but I can promise that after she does, she's not going to want to go a day without me *inside* her.

I've just got to move slow with Melissa and let her see how much her body craves me first. That's exactly why I haven't kissed her yet.

I have to prepare her for me first.

7

Ace

I T'S HALF PAST TEN AND Melissa is just walking out
of the coffee shop. She looks around for a few seconds as if she
thinks that I've left her, but smiles once she finds me parked
toward the back of the lot.

I shift my truck into drive and pull up beside her. I lean over
and push her door open before reaching out my hand for her to
grab. She's hesitant at first, but grabs it and allows me to pull her up.

There's a part of her that's still not sure if she should be alone
with me yet. That's exactly why I need to take her where I have
planned tonight . . . to soften her up toward me.

She's quiet as she shuts the door and fastens her seatbelt.

"How was work?"

I can feel her watching me as I pull out of the parking lot. "Boring as usual, but it pays the bills."

"How long have you worked there?" I pull my eyes away from the road just long enough to catch her checking out my thighs in these ripped up jeans I threw on before leaving the house. They're snug and easily show the imprint of my dick, which her gaze now seems to be focused on.

I laugh and look back up at the road. "Glad my body can be entertaining for you after a boring day at work."

"I was just thinking." She quickly turns away as if that'll make up for being caught staring at my package. "For four years now. I've had other jobs on the side, but this has been my main job for a while now. Do you have a job other than . . . you know . . ."

I let out a little chuckle and head toward the garage. "Yeah, we're actually headed there now. A mechanic. I have a little project I need to finish and thought maybe we could talk while I work."

I want Melissa to see the side of me that many don't get to see. The *me* outside of what I do with my brothers.

"You're a mechanic?" she asks, her smile widening.

"Why are you smiling so big?" I glance over at her again to see her watching the muscles in my arms flex as I grip the steering wheel.

"I don't know . . ." Her face reddens. "I guess I can just picture you all greased up, working on vehicles. "It's–"

"*Hot.*" The word leaving my mouth has her swallowing and fidgeting with her hair, as if she's turned on by what she's picturing now.

"I work on motorcycles mostly." I pull up in front of the garage and park. "I have a hard time sleeping some nights so I like to come here and work myself into exhaustion. That is, of course, when I'm not working with my brothers."

She follows me into the garage, looking around as I flip a few of the lights on. "So if my vehicle ever breaks down?"

I lean in close to her ear, causing her to slightly jump when I speak. "I'll fix it. Naked if you want."

She sucks in a breath and I walk past her, making my way to my old Harley. I reach for the stool, pulling it up for her to take a seat.

I can feel her heated gaze on me as I yank my shirt over my head and stuff into the top of my back pocket and I can tell that I have her picturing me naked now.

She sits there quietly for a long while, just watching me work, and I love just knowing that she's here with me. It has this weird warmth spreading throughout my body, making me feel at peace.

An hour passes, maybe longer, before she finally speaks.

"How long have you been a mechanic?"

I look up from my bike and wipe my hands on a towel. "Since I was fifteen. My uncle taught me to work on vehicles back when we used to stay with him off and on. It helps to clear my head sometimes and keep the demons at bay."

"It's nice having a distraction, something that you enjoy doing."

"It does." I stand up and walk over to stand in between Melissa's legs. She lets out a small moan as I cup the back of her neck and press my body against hers. "You're a distraction for me, Melissa. In a good fucking way. Feel that?"

She sucks in a small breath when I grind my erection between her legs and growl.

"Yes. Oh God, yes." Her gaze roams over my shirtless body before moving up to land on my lips. "It's kind of hard not to *feel* you, Ace. Or not to notice you. You're a distraction for me too, no matter how much I try and fight it."

"Good," I whisper.

I grip her thighs and pick her up, carrying her over to the

closest car. She lets out a little surprised gasp as I set her down onto the hood and roughly pull her toward me so that her legs are wrapped around my waist.

I watch her watching me with curious eyes and I can tell by her heavy breathing that she desperately wants me to make the next move. So I lean in and pull her bottom lip between my teeth.

She moans and wraps her arm around my neck, pulling me in closer as I give it a soft nibble before running my tongue over it.

She wants me to kiss her, but I hold back, wanting her to wait a little longer.

I want her to fucking want me as much as I want her.

I want her to fucking crave me.

But I know, and my body sure as hell knows, that I can't hold back for much longer.

Fuck, I need to get her home.

"I should get you home." I back away and run my hands through my hair in frustration.

The twisted side of me wants to fuck her on top of every vehicle in this garage and make her scream my name until her voice goes out. I want her nails in my back, making me bleed as I fill her with my long, thick cock.

I want to fucking possess every part of her body and soul until she can't even breathe without thinking about me.

My fucked-up, twisted side won't even be a concern for her once she really *feels* me.

I'm going to make sure of that . . .

8

Melissa

I FEEL KADENCE STARING AT me and finally glance at her. I am on my break with a latte in front of me, a half-eaten scone beside that, and my mind consumed with Ace.

"What?" I know she has something on her mind, and I know she'll voice it.

I lean back in the chair and cross my arms over my chest, waiting for it to come.

She stares at me for a prolonged second, maybe trying to guess what I'm thinking about, or what's really going on. Kadence is pretty perceptive, and I know that she'll figure it out without me having to say a word.

"Are you going to tell me what's going on or do you really

want me to start naming off things?"

I really don't want to talk about this on my break, but I do want to discuss it with her. With Kadence now being with Aston, she spends a lot of her time with him. And with me working more, our time together is limited.

I hate that, hate that the majority of when we see each other is at the Lockes' house. We used to do so much together, and I want that back.

"This is about Ace, isn't it?" She phrases it like a question but I can hear in her voice that she already knows the answer.

I exhale and glance around me. Even though we are semi-secluded, it still feels like a million people can hear me. Not that I care if anyone knows I have strong feelings for Ace, but I've never been one to open up about how I feel.

"You know you can trust me, right? You can tell me whatever you want."

I look into Kadence's eyes and nod. Of course I know I can trust her, but it isn't about that. It is about me finally admitting out loud how I feel and what I want, when I'm not even sure what it all means yet.

I've never done that, never been the person to open up like this. But I know I need to talk about it.

"I trust you, Kadence. It's myself I don't trust, especially where it concerns Ace." There, I said it, all but admitted that I have no self-control when it comes to a Locke brother.

This sympathetic look crosses her face and she leans forward. When she smiles I can see that she understands what I mean, how I feel. Hell, she went through the same thing.

"I'm here. I'm listening."

"I have some pretty strong feelings for Ace, and they scare me because of the type of man he is, the violence that I know he houses." I glance away, the words spilling from my mouth for the first time ever. I've thought them plenty of times, but actually saying them out loud is another thing.

"I know." Kadence says and gives me a genuine smile. "The violence and danger that the Locke brothers have within them is not something that just anyone can accept. It was hard for me at first too." She gives me another sympathetic look. "It takes a really strong woman to be with one of those boys, and we are those women, Melissa."

I nod, knowing she speaks the truth. "I guess I'm just afraid to fully give myself over. I don't know what to do."

"Is that what you want, though? I mean, do you want to give yourself over to Ace completely? Because once you do there's no going back. He won't let you go. You'll be his irrevocably."

"Maybe." This is not something I haven't thought about before and now, after I've gotten to spend some one on one time with him, the feeling has only grown stronger. The need is becoming overwhelming, even though I'm trying to fight it. "I don't know, Kadence. I think at the end of the day that's what scares me the most when I think about it. I'm afraid that if I give myself to Ace in every way imaginable, I will be his and I'm not sure I'm ready for that." I can already see the possessiveness in his eyes when he looks at me, when he touches me. It ignites something deep in my body, makes me yearn for more than I've ever wanted before. I'm confused by it, not sure if I should accept it or run the other direction. A part of me is afraid, terrified of what it means to want him, what it will mean if I give myself over.

A part of me fears that, but another part, a bigger one, anticipates and wants it so damn badly. It's that part that's dominating me, controlling me . . . consuming me.

"Look. I'm going to be honest with you about something,

Melissa. And listen carefully."

I sit up straight, nervous to hear what she's going say. Especially since it will undoubtedly involve Ace. "Okay," I say a little hesitantly. Kadence can be a little abrasive when she wants her point made. But I love her because of it. Hell, right now maybe that's what I need. "Give it to me."

"All right . . ." She sits up straight too now. "Ace is twisted in ways that his brothers aren't. It's simply because he went through hell the longest and had to stand up and become the Locke that his younger brothers could look up to for protection. But I know without a doubt that Ace or any of the other brothers would never hurt someone they care about, especially a woman. They protect those who need it. It may be scary giving your heart and body over to a Locke, but I can tell you with everything in me that it's the best feeling in the world once the initial fear wears off. It's even exciting in ways that you've never experienced before. At least it was with Aston for me. I can't even imagine what it'd be like with Ace."

I feel my stomach sink because I hate to hear how Ace and his brothers were forced into becoming who they are today by parents who physically hurt them and put them in danger. I've heard some of the stories and they're ugly and unimaginable. It's one of the reasons I've softened toward Ace a bit. Because no one should have to go through what they went through. "I know Ace would never physically hurt me, Kadence. It's not the physical part that I'm worried about. Everything about him is so damn intense."

"Well, you shouldn't be worried about him hurting you in any way. When the Locke brothers find someone they care about, they never stop loving them." She smiles as if just remembering something. "Oh, and I almost forgot that Sterling and Wynter are having a fire at their house tonight. You're coming. Ace is coming. The whole crew is coming. It's going to be great."

I feel my heart speed up at the thought of seeing Ace again so soon. Truthfully, I haven't stopped thinking about him since he dropped me back off at my car last night.

The moment he set me down onto the car and pressed his hard body between my legs, I almost forgot how to breathe. Especially when he pulled my bottom lip between his teeth. That scared me even more.

If he could make me feel that way simply by touching me . . . I can't even begin to imagine how he'd make me feel if he kissed me.

I've dreamt about those sexy lips on my body more times than I can even count and I know for a fact that I'd be done for the moment I feel them owning me. Because I know that's what he'd do.

He'd own me with just a single kiss and I need to make sure I can handle being his before I allow that to happen.

"Do I have a choice?"

She shakes her head and stands up. "Nope. You're family. If you even think about not showing up, you'll have one of the Lockes at your door, breaking it down."

"I don't doubt it," I huff.

And I'm sure Ace would look sexy as hell doing it too . . .

Ace

I LEAN AGAINST BOBBY'S DOOR and pull out the rest of the joint that's stuffed inside my jacket pocket and light it up. "Don't make me bust this door down, Bobster . . ." Placing it between my lips, I light it and take a few quick hits, keeping the smoke in my lungs for a second before blowing it out. I glance down at my watch. "I've got somewhere to be. That means you have about twenty fucking seconds to unlock this door before I break it down, come inside, and drag you out by your fucking balls."

"Ten seconds now . . ."

I hear the clicking of the handle unlock, and then a second later the sound of footsteps running through the house comes through.

"Really?" I flick the rest of the joint across the porch before I speed walk around the house and to the back door. This idiot tried this shit last time. You'd think he'd know it's pointless for him to run from me.

As soon as I round the corner, I get a clear view of Bobby jumping off the back porch and racing for some shitty little bicycle that's laying in the yard.

"This is pretty fucking comical, Bobster." I watch as his overweight ass struggles with the little bike but gets nowhere.

"Shit!" He screams as it falls over.

"Chasing you is like chasing a toddler." I make my way over and stand above him as he struggles with getting back up. "Why do you insist on running every damn time? Is it simply for my entertainment or is it because you really believe you'll get away?"

"I don't have the money," he spits out, kicking the bike away. "I told Jim I'd have it next week. Can't you just give me a break, buddy? Come on . . . I promise I'll have it by next Friday."

For a second I just stare at Bobby, and although I'm pissed at this little fucker because he owes me money, I can't help but start to chuckle at the comical routine he always delivers.

This isn't the first time I've had to chase his ass around, but in the grand scheme of things he's harmless.

He's a dirty bastard, and I mean that in a literal sense. Overweight from only eating fast food, and reeking of cheap-ass beer, Bobby's always getting himself in shit.

And I'm the stupid motherfucker who lets him get away with it.

I should just put a stop to it, but because of all the dark shit I've gone through—and still go through—this is almost like a little reprieve from all of that.

"Get up, Bobby." I take a step back as he tries to stand upright. His white shirt is stained with grease, and the hem hits him right above his bulging stomach. He's even got some fucking lint in his belly button.

I just shake my head at the state he's in. He's a sorry sack of shit, that's for sure.

"I'm sorry, Ace. I swear I'll have your money next week. I swear it." He starts crying over and over again, sweat starting to cover his forehead and dripping down his temples. He needs to calm the fuck down or he'll have a heart attack. "I'm really, really sorry—"

I reach out and slap him across the face. His fat cheek jiggles and he stumbles back a little bit. His face instantly becomes red and I know that he's going to start crying any second. I don't have time for him to be apologizing continuously.

He's panting, breathing like he just ran a fucking marathon. "Calm the hell down, Bobby." I cross my arms over my chest and eye him up and down. The asshole is out of shape. If he wants to fuck over people then he should at least work out so he can get away. "Because I'm in a good fucking mood, I'll give you three days to get me my money." He opens his mouth as if he wants to argue, or maybe tell me again how he needs a week, but I hold my hand up and give him a hard fucking look. "No, you have three motherfucking days to get me my money. If you don't I'm gonna come back here and I'm going to open you up like a goddamn fish. Do you understand me?"

He starts nodding furiously, and then starts repeating over and over how thankful he is. I turn, leaving him standing there, wondering why the fuck I let him off the hook.

On any other day I wouldn't have given him a second chance. But the truth is I *am* in a good mood, the thought of Melissa still running through my head. Although I will never change who I am, or how I do things, even knowing that Melissa can soon be mine has me feeling . . . different. I don't know if I like it, but I sure as hell don't want it to disappear.

I head back to the truck and climb in, and for a second I just sit there, staring out in the distance and thinking about Melissa. She's all I've been thinking about lately, but hell, I like that. I want her on my mind always. I want her by my fucking side. It is hard as hell not to just make her see that she's mine. But I don't want to rush this, don't want her to see me as some arrogant fucking bastard who can't keep his dick in his pants.

But the truth is I want her so damn badly. I want her under me, naked. I want her arms above her head, her breasts thrust out as she parts her thighs. I want her begging me for more. And I want to bury my face between her legs and lick her pussy until she comes in my mouth.

I reach down and adjust my massive erection, groaning at the very image of me thrusting in and out of Melissa. Fuck, I'm so damn aroused, so ready to claim her and make her mine. And I know that time will come, sooner rather than later. I'm a patient man, but when it comes to Melissa I want her like a fucking fiend jonesing for his next fix.

Shit, I need to get control of myself. I can't be going off the handle. This isn't like me, isn't how I operate.

I want Melissa like I want to fucking breathe. I want her as mine, forever, with nothing stopping me, no one telling me that she isn't mine. I want her to see we belong together, that we've always belonged together. She's afraid, I see that, but I'll show her that if she were mine she'd be treated like a fucking queen.

I am coming to realize that when it comes to Melissa, all bets are off on how things play out. I am so not in my element with her, but I like it.

I fucking love it.

Melissa

I GOT OFF WORK HOURS ago, but took the time to decide if I should make an appearance at Sterling and Wynter's or not, knowing that I'd be seeing Ace there.

Yet, when I arrived thirty minutes ago, and everyone was here but him, I couldn't help but to be filled with disappointment.

I've been sitting beside Kadence and Aston, and although Kadence has been making attempts to talk to me every few minutes, my mind has been too distracted to pay attention to anything she's been saying. The way Kadence is with Aston makes me long for that with Ace, and a part of me hates myself for wanting that, knowing the type of man he is. He's dangerous, but not to me. Never to me. He helps people, even if that is violent, destructive. But that's the way he is, who he is. I wouldn't want to change him ever.

I keep finding myself staring out into the darkened street waiting for Ace to show up. Hoping he'll show up.

"Why is your leg bouncing?"

"Huh?" I pull my gaze away from the road and take a sip of the beer in my hand. "It's not. What are you talking about?"

She just laughs and places her hand on my knee, stopping it from moving. "Why are you acting all weird?"

"I'm not. What do you mean?"

"Okay . . . if you're not acting weird then why have you ignored everything everyone has said to you since you got here?" She looks out toward the street at the same time I find myself doing it again. "Ah . . . I see."

I shake my head and let out a small laugh. "What is that supposed to mean?"

"Oh, never mind." She's silent for a moment. "But Ace isn't coming."

My heart sinks in unwanted disappointment. "I thought you said he was?"

She shakes her head and reaches for her beer. "He got held up with a job and said not to expect him tonight." I feel like this weight settles on me, holding me down. He's not coming tonight, and that makes me feel like shit. I realize, even if I want to hide it, try to pretend to myself that it's not true, that I am well and deeply into Ace and there's no going back.

She smiles as she takes in my disappointment. "You wanted to see him, didn't you?" Her voice rises and I have to shush her before everyone else hears.

"I don't know what would make you think that. I never once said that."

"Really?" She pauses for a second before speaking again. "Look up."

"What for . . ." I look up and my breath gets sucked right from my lungs at the sight of Ace walking through the yard right toward us with King at his side.

He's here. I feel like that weight is gone, that I can breathe easier now. I don't know if that feeling should scare the fuck out of me or not.

He's wearing that damn baseball cap again, and the way his intense gaze is trained on me as if he wants to devour me right where I sit, has me squeezing the beer bottle tighter.

I find myself looking away.

Ace keeps walking straight toward me, and before I know it, he's kneeling in front of me and grabbing the beer from my hand.

He doesn't say anything as his gaze meets mine and he tilts the beer back, drinking half of it in one go. When he pulls the bottle away, a little bit spills on his lips and I can't help but notice how sexy it is when he wipes it away with his tongue.

"Vanilla," he whispers with a twisted little grin, leaning in close to smell my lips. "You probably shouldn't wear that on your lips unless you want me to lick it off."

He stands and winks before walking into the house and leaving me sitting here with my damn heart practically beating out of my chest with excitement at the idea of his tongue on my lips again.

Ace Locke is so sexy that I can hardly handle it.

I'm so caught up in what he just said that it takes me a few seconds to realize that he never gave me my beer back.

He's good at getting what he wants, so I don't doubt that he did it on purpose to lure me away from everyone, but still I find myself doing what I do next, feeling like I *need* to.

"I need another beer." I stand up and wipe my sweaty palms down the front of my jeans, my nervousness claiming me, taking hold, refusing to get control. "I'll be right back."

I swallow down my nerves and make my way into the house, fully aware that Ace could be hiding somewhere in the darkness, waiting for the moment I step into his trap.

With my heart racing, I walk through the kitchen and, just as I'm about to turn down the hallway, Ace backs me against the wall, closing me in with his strong body.

My breathing picks up when his rough hands grab my wrists and pin them against the wall above me.

Silently, he watches me, as if he's trying to figure me out.

He slowly moves in closer, teasing me with his lips close to mine, but stops before there's any contact. His mouth twists into a satisfied grin when he notices my chest quickly rising and falling. The anticipation of what he's going to do next moves through my veins.

Closing his eyes, he squeezes my wrists tighter and gently runs the tip of his tongue over my lips, tasting me.

"You didn't take it off . . ."

I find myself breathless as I attempt to speak. "Didn't have any reason to . . ."

"Fucking good, Angel."

Slowly, he lowers one of his hands down my arm until he moves it around to grip my throat and lightly squeeze.

It's then that I feel his massive erection pressing against my belly.

I should attempt to get away, leave before I no longer have that option, but I don't.

Instead, I close my eyes and moan out as he thrusts his hips further against me, completely unashamed that my taste has aroused him.

"That's all I needed to hear . . ."

He releases my throat long enough to yank his cap off and toss it aside. Then he squeezes my throat a little harder than before. His actions have me breathing so heavily that he lets out a small laugh before he speaks against my lips. "Don't go passing out on me, Angel. We haven't even gotten to the good stuff yet."

As soon as he speaks the last word, he sucks my bottom lip into his sexy mouth, causing me to moan out and grip at his muscled arm, digging my nails in.

His teasing has my body on edge, about ready to explode just from the anticipation alone.

But I have a feeling he already knows this, because he seems to be enjoying it a hell of a lot. This is even more torturous than last night.

With his mouth still on mine, he moves down to grip my thighs, pulling me up so that my legs are wrapped around his waist.

The feel of his erection has me so turned on that I accidently moan out his name.

This has his lips twisting into a smirk. "My name sounds damn good coming from your mouth, Angel. I can't wait to make you scream it."

My heart thunders, beating hard, like a war drum in my chest. I need to get myself under control.

"Are you two coming back . . . whoa . . . whoa . . . am I inter-rupting something here?"

I push my way out of Ace's arms at the sound of my best friend's voice. Once I have my thoughts clear, I look over to see Kadence smiling at me over the top of her beer bottle. I purse my lips. I know I won't live this down. "No," I say pathetically. "We were just grabbing some beers. You need another one? I'll grab it." I can hear myself rambling and I know my face is probably so damn red.

Clearing my throat, I squeeze by Ace's hard body, which hasn't moved an inch since I wiggled my way out of his arms, and move over to the fridge, opening it. My heart is pounding relentlessly as I reach for two beers, grab Kadence's arm and quickly pull her outside, away from Ace.

"Looks like you two have been having a little more fun than you mentioned to me earlier."

"Shut it," I whisper. "We haven't done anything."

"Yet," she says with a small laugh as we take our seats by the fire again. "Ace is going to erase the worries from your mind completely and soon you won't even care about his dangerous side. You'll crave it. Just wait."

I know she's not wrong about that and it terrifies me that he has the power to do that.

Ace Locke has the power to own me completely and he's barely even touched me yet . . .

11

Ace

I CAN'T HELP BUT GRIN as I watch Melissa leave the house. She's embarrassed that Kadence saw what we were doing. Hell, I don't care if anybody watches, if anybody sees what I was doing with the woman I care about, with the woman I want as mine.

I'll show every fucking asshole on this planet who has doubts that Melissa is mine. And she is, all of her.

She's mine. There's no doubt about that, no going around it.

Never in my life have I gone slowly, refrained from going after what I want. But with Melissa I'm taking my time. I want her to be right there with me, primed and ready for what I have to give her.

I walk over to the door and lean against the frame, staring out the screen and watching Melissa. She sits down in front of the fire, her body tense, the taste of her still on my lips. I reach out and adjust my cock, the bastard thick and long, painful.

My body knows she's mine, and it reacts accordingly. My heart races, my muscles tense, and my cock gets harder than fucking steel. Just one look at her and I'm ready to go.

Damn, I want her so fucking badly. I want her on my bed, want to spread her thighs and devour her pussy. I know she'll taste so sweet.

As slow as I am going, it is damn torture. But I can tell she is right here with me, wanting the same things I do. But I want her to know that she has control. I want her to see that I will never push her.

I feel myself smile as I watch her tip her head back and laugh. This isn't just about sex where Melissa is concerned. I want her by my side. I want to defend her because she is mine, want to tell everyone that if they mess with her they'll deal with me.

She looks back and our gazes clash. I smile and she returns the gesture. I want to go out there, pick her up, throw her over my shoulder and take her upstairs to a spare room.

Hell, I have no idea why I am refraining from doing just that. Maybe she sees my expression and knows what I am thinking, or maybe she wants the same thing, but a second later she stands and starts walking back toward the house, while Kadence is distracted by my brother.

I open the front door and move to the side so she can come in. And then I take her hand and lead her upstairs; neither of us saying anything, both of us knowing exactly what is going to happen.

Maybe we'll have sex. Maybe I'll be able to claim her for the first time, something I've wanted to do since the moment I met her. Or maybe I'll just hold her and listen to the sound of her breathing, knowing that she is here with me, bringing me pleasure with her company alone . . . bringing me peace.

I don't really give a shit one way or the other what we do, because she is here with me and that's all that I care about.

Once we reach the top of the stairs, I guide her down to the end of the hall, where I know there's a spare bedroom.

For what I have planned I don't want anyone to interrupt us.

But before I open the door, I pin her up against it with my body, as I lean in close and brush my lips up her neck, stopping below her ear. "Are you sure you want to be alone with me right now, Angel?" I whisper, my voice this husky growl of need. "Once we step inside this room, I can't promise that I won't taste you where I really want to. Where I was holding back from last night."

I feel her shiver in response as I run my tongue along her neck, giving her a feel of how badly I want it on her body.

"I'll twist you up with my tongue alone," I whisper. "I'll make you come undone before you even have time to hit the mattress."

Without saying a word, she nods, giving me permission to go forward.

Fuck, how I love that.

Keeping her against the door, I lower my way down her body and grip the top of her jeans, yanking them down until they hit the floor.

Her standing there, the wet spot I can see between her legs, her arousal soaking her panties, has me practically ripping them down her legs before I lift her up to straddle my face.

I can hear her heavy breathing as she grips my hair, the anticipation of me tasting her working her up.

"Hold onto me tighter. You're not gonna want to let go."

Her hold on my hair tightens and a long moan leaves her lips the moment I flick my tongue out and run it along her wet pussy, tasting her.

Fuck, I want to own her flavor. I want to make it mine and mine alone.

It will be. She'll always be mine. Only mine.

I won't hesitate to kill any motherfucker who thinks he has a right to her taste ever again.

She moans again as I bury my face further between her legs, shoving my tongue inside her to memorize her flavor.

"That's right, Angel. Moan for me. It makes me so fucking hard."

The combination of my words and tongue has her crying out and gripping my hair as if her life depends on it.

"Ace . . ." I feel her legs squeeze my head as I continue to lick and flick at her pretty cunt, hitting her right where I know she needs it. "Keep going . . . keep . . . yes . . . yes . . ."

I growl out against her pussy, the vibration of my mouth causing her to squeeze my head so tightly that I can barely breathe. Even that doesn't stop me from licking until she's coming undone around my face, her release tasting on my tongue.

Needing a moment to breathe, I press her back against the wall and hold her there until her grip on my hair loosens and her breathing evens out.

Then I slowly lower her down the wall, setting her on her feet.

"Holy fuck . . . what just happened?"

"The beginning of me showing you that you're mine." I grip her face and lean it back before sucking her bottom lip into my mouth and growling. "I'm not sure you're ready for what's to come next."

She's still fighting to catch her breath when Kadence calls her name from the kitchen.

This has her cussing under her breath and moving away from

me. "My clothes. I need my clothes."

Keeping my gaze on her, I reach for her panties and help her slide them up her legs, before doing the same with her jeans. "I want to spend time with you soon. I'm busy tomorrow night, but I'm free on Friday. I'll pick you up after work."

She just looks at me as if she doesn't know what to say before nodding. "Okay. Yeah, I get off at seven."

I smile and stand back and watch as she takes shaky steps down the stairs, being careful that her legs don't give out on her.

Pride fucking fills me that it's because of me that she's having a hard time walking right.

If she thinks it's hard to move now, she hasn't felt anything yet. Once I'm inside of her all bets are off.

I have a feeling she won't be leaving my bed for days . . .

12

Melissa

I T FELT STRANGE, KADENCE BEING the one to grill me last night about a Locke brother. She kept trying to get me to confess to doing something *naughty* with Ace, but I kept denying it, not ready to confess yet.

I finally managed to call it a night, before I could manage to spend the rest of it drooling over Ace from across the yard.

Every single time he looked at me, I felt my insides burst into flames at the reminder of him tasting me.

I've never had such an intense orgasm in my entire life and I feel as if I'm still recovering from it.

Just the thought of his lips and tongue sends my body over the edge with this powerful need.

That's exactly why I need to reconsider allowing Ace to pick me up tomorrow night. I said yes without even thinking and now I can't *stop* thinking of excuses I should've come up with.

" . . . some pretty hot guys here. What do you think about that one?"

I focus my attention on Gia long enough to catch the end of what she's saying. She's pointing at some pretty boy from across the bar and although he's cute, I can't help but to compare him to Ace.

I compare all guys to Ace, it seems. Maybe that makes me crazy, but it's inevitable anymore.

"He's okay." I shrug and take a sip of my drink.

"What do you mean okay?" Gia gives me a strange look. "Do you need glasses or something? That man is *fine* and so is his friend."

I turn away from Gia and give the guy a second glance before turning my attention to his friend. "I guess. I don't know." I spin the stool back around to face the bar. "Let's just focus on our drink. I'm not here to check out guys. I just want to unwind a little."

"That might be a problem now," she says in a voice mixed with excitement and nervousness. "They're coming this way and his friend's attention is on you."

Just great.

I exhale, squeeze my eyes shut, and pray I can make them leave without them giving me a hard time.

A few months ago, I would've been excited at the opportunity to meet an attractive guy and possibly get to know him. I haven't dated anyone since Jordan and I broke up two years ago and I've missed having a companion in my life. But no one has ever piqued my interest long enough for me to give them a chance, to allow them in my life.

That is, until Ace came along.

He is a bad boy, rough around the edges, and something in me feels alive around him. I want to feel that danger and violence that I know radiates from him, covers him like a second skin. I want to feel like, with him, I'm on the edge of this cliff and not even caring if I fall over and never reach the bottom.

And I do feel like that when I'm with him. He's the only one who has ever made me want more.

But now, the idea of meeting some random guy in a bar doesn't sound the least bit appealing. Especially when all I can think about is Ace and how it felt when he made me come; the way his mouth felt so amazing on me. There's no way I'll be able to focus on some other guy when physically he doesn't even compare to Ace.

"Ladies. Can we buy you two some new drinks?"

I keep my attention straight ahead, not speaking, not even acknowledging them. I know if I do they'll get the wrong idea. They usually do. I'm trying to think of the best way to get out of this situation without upsetting Gia. I know she's attracted to the dark-haired guy and there's no way I can leave her here alone with two strange men.

"Sure. I'd love one," she says happily.

My stomach twists into nervous knots, not knowing what to expect from this night now.

I force a smile and turn around to face the two of them. The friend is taller and thicker, with light hair and a cleanshaven face. He's cute, but does nothing for me. "I'm good, but thank you."

The dark-haired guy's friend nods and takes a seat next to me. I hear the scraping of the stool as he scoots it closer to me, but I keep my focus on something else so that he doesn't get the wrong idea.

I can feel him watching me and it's making me uncomfortable, but I do my best to ignore the feeling so that Gia can get a chance to at least get her guy's number.

"Where is your ring?"

"Excuse me?" I pull my glass away from my mouth and look beside me.

"Your ring?" The friend says with a cocky grin. "I don't see a ring on your finger, yet you're refusing a drink from me. That's not something that happens to me often."

Great, he's one of those guys. If he'd been decent he wouldn't have mentioned anything about me not accepting a drink from him. At least from my experience that's how it usually goes.

"I don't need a ring to refuse a drink from a stranger," I say stiffly. "I'm good with the one I have. I appreciate the offer."

Feeling uncomfortable, I turn my attention to my left to see Gia laughing and talking with the other guy. Clearly, she's forgotten that I didn't even want them coming over here.

"Come on," he pushes. "Our friends seem to be hitting it off. Let me buy you a drink and we can talk. What you're sipping on is practically just juice. It's not going to get you drunk."

"I'm good," I say tightly, removing his hand as he places it on my leg. "Save your money and your time. Just because our friends are getting to know each other doesn't mean we need to."

"You know . . ." He grabs my arm and squeezes it when I go to reach for my drink again. "You're being a real bitch when all I'm trying to do is–"

Before he can finish what he's saying, his head is being slammed into the bar in front of him with so much force that my glass shakes and falls over.

I feel my eyes widen as I look up to see Ace standing there. He's the one who has a grip on the back of the asshole's hair and from the look on his face, he doesn't plan on letting him up anytime soon.

My heart drops to my stomach as his intense gaze turns to meet mine. There's this animalistic quality inside of his eyes, reminding me of just how dangerous and unpredictable he is.

It somewhat scares me, yet I can't turn away from him.

It also turns me on.

There's something incredibly sexy about Ace when he's angry.

With a growl, he pulls the guy's head back and whispers, "Touch her again and I'll cut your scalp off with the knife I have shoved inside my boot. It won't be the first time I've played that fucking game and enjoyed it." After he pulls his lips away he slams his head down again, not once, but two times, before he releases his hair and steps back.

The guy that Gia is talking to stands tall, as if to come to his friend's defense, but suddenly takes a step back and throws his hands up in defense once Ace steps up to him with a tilt of his head.

The look in his eyes screams that he'll kill anyone who challenges him, and that is enough to keep everyone at a distance, including the guy whose mouth is now covered in blood from his nose, which Ace just busted.

Everyone in the bar seems to be watching Ace as he steps in close to me and cups the back of my head with force. "This is not the place for you to be hanging out at. There's drunken assholes everywhere."

"How did you . . ." I shake my head and stand up when he grabs my waist. "How did you know I was here? I thought you were busy tonight."

"I was," he says on an angry growl. "I got done early and asked Kadence where you were. It's a good thing too, because if this motherfucker would've gotten any further with you, I'd have to do much worse to him than I just did."

As if no one else is in the room, Ace presses his body flush against mine and leans in to speak against my lips. "I'm fighting with everything in me to not turn back around and kill that asshole for touching you the way he did. *Leave* with me before I lose my willpower."

I take a step back and swallow. His closeness has my heart racing so fast that I can hardly catch my breath. "I can't. I'm here with a friend."

"Looks like she's ready to leave too." He glances over my shoulder, his eyes narrowed as if to give a warning.

That's all it takes for the dark-haired guy to walk away from Gia and leave her standing there staring at me.

"What the . . ." I can't tell if she's mad or just in shock at the fact that I'm standing here with Ace right now. "I should get going anyway. It's late. I'll see you at work tomorrow."

"Gia!" I call out her name as she quickly walks away, but she doesn't stop to look back at me. I look around at all the attention on me and suddenly feel as if I need some air.

I barely make it outside before I feel Ace's hands on my waist, gripping me from behind as he moves his body in close.

He's hard all over, and as much as I crave to feel him against me, my head is screaming at me to run from him. Tonight was just too much . . . too real. I need to think, to breathe and collect myself.

I feel like this was a warning sign, reminding me before it's too late that falling for Ace could be disastrous.

"I'll walk." I take a deep breath and find the courage to walk away from him, but the moment he stops me again and his breath hits my neck, I feel weak again and I want nothing more than to give in and leave with him. "It's not that far, Ace. I'll be fine."

"It's too far for me to let you walk alone. I wouldn't give a shit if it was right behind this place. You're not going anywhere alone tonight." He brushes my hair away from my neck and runs his lips along it. "Come with me, Angel."

My breathing picks up and, just like usual, I can't control my thoughts when he's so damn close to me. I should be walking away from him, yet I can't seem to.

"I want to but . . ."

"But what?"

"Was that true?"

He lets out a deep, throaty laugh that vibrates my ear. "Is what true?"

"That you once scalped a guy?"

He's tense, but then I feel him nod before he speaks the words. "Yes. That wasn't just a threat. I'd do it to that asshole inside in a heartbeat if he ever touched you again. That's a fucking promise."

His confession makes it hard for me to breathe. Hard for me to move and before I know it, I'm allowing him to guide toward the motorcycle I watched him work on the other night.

I stand frozen, watching his biceps flex as he reaches for his helmet and slides it on my head. Ace is completely hypnotizing and in this moment, I feel as if I'll do *anything* he tells me to.

He takes a moment to look me over, maybe seeing how I look wearing his helmet, before he straddles the motorcycle and grabs my hand, pulling me on behind him.

"Hold on tight. I have somewhere I want to show you." He grabs my arms and places them around his body when I don't make a move. "Don't let go."

I finally snap out of it and lean into him, while holding onto his firm body as tightly as I can.

Once I've got a good grip on him, he takes off, heading toward an area I've never been in before.

We ride for a good fifteen minutes before pulling up to an old abandoned building that looks like it hasn't been used in ages.

My heart races with anticipation as he helps me off the bike and leads me into the old place.

"My brothers and I spent a lot of time here when we were

kids. When my uncle wasn't around to save us . . ." He opens the door and turns to face me. "I had to. This was the only place I knew we'd be safe."

I feel my heart sink at his confession as I follow him inside.

He doesn't move at first. He just stands in place and looks around as if being here is bringing up old memories.

"There's a room I want to show you." His jaw flexes as he grabs my hand and gives it a light squeeze. "I feel like I need to put it to use right now."

I'm not sure what he means by *putting it to use,* but I allow him to pull me through the darkened house anyway.

"Your parents hurt you and your brothers a lot, didn't they?"

He stops and takes a deep breath before pushing one of the hallway doors open and stepping into the room. "Almost every fucking day."

"I hate that," I admit. "I hate that they hurt you guys. It's not fair."

"It's not," he says stiffly, turning on a few lanterns to give the room some light. "That's why I made this."

I turn to face the wall when he nods toward it. There's a huge target painted onto a piece of plywood that has huge chunks missing from it. You can tell it's gotten a lot of use over the years.

"Was this for you and your brothers to let off some steam?"

He shakes his head and kneels down to reach into his boot. "It was for me."

I jump when he quickly stands up and throws a knife into the target, hitting the bullseye.

His heated gaze lands on me and I can tell that he must notice how nervous I look now that he's got a knife.

I'm alone in an old abandoned building with a pissed-off Locke, a knife and a target.

I should probably be more nervous than I am, but the moment he pulls the knife from the target and hands it to me, I relax as I look down at it in my hand.

Ace is showing me a piece of *him* and I'm going to take every last bit of that I can get . . .

13

Ace

I SAW THE WAY MELISSA stiffened when I pulled the knife from my boot and threw it at the target. There was a split second that I hated she was afraid I could harm her.

I'd never hurt her, never even dream of it. Hell, I'd kill, maim anyone who thought of putting fear in her.

It fucking kills me and I want to give her every reason to know that she'll *always* be safe with me.

"Throw it at the target, Melissa." She pulls her gaze away from the knife to look up at me. "If anyone has ever hurt you, they're that fucking target. Throw it."

"I've never been hurt enough by anyone to want them to be the target, Ace." She brushes past me to stand where I was just moments ago when I threw it. "But I'll be more than happy to pretend it's your parents."

Before I can say anything or react to the fact that she hates my parents so much for hurting us, she throws the knife at the target but misses it, hitting the wall beside it.

"Here." I walk over and pull the knife out of the wall before I make my way back over to her. "Don't think so much next time. Just relax and aim."

She takes the knife from me as I hand it to her.

I stand back and watch as she throws it again. A satisfied smile spreads across her face when it hits the target this time.

I fetch the knife and allow her to throw it a few more times. She seems to be enjoying it more with each throw and I can't help but to get turned on by watching her.

As much as I'm enjoying watching her let loose, I still can't get that look of fear that was in her eyes when I grabbed my knife out of my head.

She throws the knife one last time, but instead of handing it to her and stepping away, this time I hand it to her and back her against the wall.

"I'll never fucking hurt you, Melissa. I *need* you to know that."

Keeping her pressed against the wall with my body, I grab the back of my shirt and pull it over my head. I toss it aside and look down to see her breathing heavily, her gaze roaming over my body.

"I wasn't afraid of you hurting me, Ace. I'm just in an unfamiliar place and the knife caught me off guard . . ."

Her words trail off when I grab her hand and place the blade of the knife to my chest. "I'd let you cut me before I ever let any harm come your way. I'll always fucking protect you." I stare into her eyes, seeing them grow wider, her shock, maybe even a little bit of fear of the situation, claiming her. But I can also see she knows the truth, can see it in her expression. "Now. Cut me."

She shakes her head and attempts to pull the knife away from my chest, but I push it farther into my skin, drawing blood. "Ace— stop. I don't want to hurt . . ."

I move her hand along my body, digging the blade in, stopping at my collarbone. "I've never let anyone cut me before," I say, my voice a low growl. "That's how much I trust you and *need* you to trust me back."

Once I release her hand, she tosses the knife aside and runs the tips of her fingers over my wound. "I trust you, Ace. I know you won't physically hurt me. But I'm not sure I'm ready for the things you do. The violence you bring to others. I don't–"

"Touch me, Angel." I place my hand on hers and lower it down the top of my jeans. "Let loose and forget about everything else for once. Fucking touch me." I bow my head and run my tongue across her lips. "Take my cock out and stroke it until I come in your hands."

She releases a sharp breath when I lower her hand to my erection. She looks surprised at how hard I am after what I just made her do to me.

"The pain doesn't bother me," I whisper against her lips. "You can hurt me all you want and I'll still be hard and ready for you. *Always.*"

I lean my head back and close my eyes as Melissa's hands work on undoing my jeans. Our heavy breathing is the only noise in the room and I love that she can't control hers, just as I can't mine.

The moment her hand touches my bare cock, I bite my bottom lip and growl out my need for her. "Stroke me like you want to . . . like you *own* me, because you do."

With a small moan, she begins stroking me, her breathing picking up as if she can hardly handle the fact that she's pleasuring me.

I place my hands against the wall on either side of her head and watch as she runs both her hands over my long, thick cock.

Each time her fingers move over my head, I moan, feeling like I could come any second. She moans too once she notices the drop of pre-cum wetting the tip of my cock.

"I'm so fucking close, Angel. Squeeze tighter."

She squeezes me tighter, using the moisture from the head of my cock to make her strokes slicker and faster.

I growl and grip the wall, feeling a tug at my balls. I'm so fucking close and she's barely touched me.

But it's not about the way it feels to have her stroking me, although it feels fantastic. It's about the fact that she *is* stroking me that has me ready to fucking explode.

I've wanted Melissa's hands on me for as long as I can remember and knowing that she's enjoying it just as much as I am is enough to send me over the edge.

"Fuck, yes . . ." I thrust my hips forward and move my hands down to wrap into the back of her hair as her strokes become faster and harder.

"Holy shit, Ace," she breathes. "I want you to come for me. I want to see you get off."

"Fuck!" Her words send me over the edge and within seconds, I'm busting my nut all over her hands as she continues to move them over my length, making sure to get every last drop out.

I fight to catch my breath as I grab her chin and tilt it up so that she's looking me in the eye. "Next time I bust . . . it will be inside your tight little pussy, Angel."

Her body shivers from my words as if just the thought is too much for her to handle. It makes my dick jump with excitement. "Ace . . . this is not what I expected tonight. I don't usually–"

"Pleasure twisted, homicidal maniacs?" I cup her face and

move in closer when she removes her hands from me. "There's a first time for everything," I breathe. "But I can promise that it won't be your last."

I move in and press my lips against hers, kissing her gently at first before deepening the kiss, until she's fighting for air.

Then I move away and grab my shirt to clean her hands off with.

She watches me in silence, her gaze raking over me, as I take care of her. I may do a lot of damage with my hands, but I can be gentle with them when needed.

After she's all cleaned up, I toss my shirt aside again and move in so that our bodies are flush. I slowly move my hands up her body, stopping once I reach the back of her hair. "It's late. I should get you home. I just wanted to show you this place first."

She swallows and nods. "Okay, yeah . . ." Her words trail off as she moves around me and heads for the door.

I stand here for a few moments, taking deep breaths before I follow her outside and help her back onto my bike.

The last place I want to take her is home, because it's not *my* fucking home, where she belongs.

I can feel that she's so damn close to where I need her to be and that is enough for tonight. Soon, though, I know what I have to do to really get her to where I need her.

I just need a little more time to show her that I'm more than just the twisted Locke she's feared since the moment she's heard about us.

Melissa

I'VE BEEN AT THE COFFEE shop for seven hours now and the *only* thing I have been able to think about is Ace Locke. Truthfully, I haven't been able to stop thinking about him since the moment he dropped me off at my house and drove off on his motorcycle last night.

I knew if I allowed Ace to touch me, to kiss me and taste me, that I'd be completely consumed by him. Yet I allowed him to do those things anyway, because a part of me wanted to know what it'd feel like to give myself over to him.

To give him a piece of me that I know I can never get back.

He hasn't even slept with me yet, but he doesn't have to for me to *feel* the way that I do about him. My feelings for him have slowly been growing with each moment we spend together and the fact that he took me somewhere so personal to him last night has my walls slowly crumbling down.

But it doesn't change the fact that I'm not sure if I'm ready for Ace's lifestyle and everything that comes along with it.

The violence.

The blood.

The worry.

We're not even *together,* but I find myself worrying about him. I'm terrified he'll get hurt or even killed and the idea of that makes me sick to my stomach.

After having his perfect mouth on me . . . and his rough, dangerous hands, I feel as if I'll go crazy without him touching me. I want him to touch me all the time and now that I've touched *him* . . . made him come for me, I'm addicted to the rush he gives me.

The sound that came from his throat when I made him come undone has haunted me all day, making me imagine him making that noise above me, buried deep inside me. I'm so wet, ready for him, primed in ways I've never even dreamed of. Only Ace can make me feel unraveled. I want more, so much more, but I'm afraid to ask for it, frightened to even imagine how real that would be.

Once that transpires, once I allow that to happen, I'll be *his* and there will be *no* going back. I know this without a doubt.

And a part of me wants that.

My shift is over soon and I haven't decided where I should go yet once I get off. I could go home and spend the entire night thinking about the one man I *shouldn't* be falling for, or I could show up at the Locke house to see him.

Every part of me wants to see him. Wants to *feel* him despite the worry I still possess.

"What's your plans for tonight?"

I look up from cleaning the counter at the sound of Gia's voice. She hasn't mentioned last night yet, but I can tell she's been wanting to since the moment I walked through the door.

"I'm not sure yet. I may just go home and watch TV."

She crosses her arms over her chest and leans against the counter as I continue to clean. "Are you just going to pretend that the scariest Locke didn't show up at the bar last night and break a guy's face over you?"

I swallow and look up to see her studying me. "Ace is over-protective and that *guy* wouldn't stop pushing me to accept a drink from him. He wanted to get me drunk, Gia. I'm not sure I feel sorry for him."

Her face softens. "I'm sorry. I had no idea he was pushing you. I was too wrapped up in Rye. I should've been paying more attention instead of putting you in an uncomfortable situation."

I shrug and toss the towel into the sink. "It's fine. I'm actually pretty happy that Ace showed up when he did. He's not as bad as you think . . . None of them are, Gia. They're just . . ."

"Misunderstood," she says with a small smile. "I guess I can see that. Plus, they're completely gorgeous. All three of them. Maybe I should've landed myself a Locke."

We both laugh, but stop and look over when the bell on the door chimes.

The moment my gaze sets on Ace, who steps inside dressed in a white Henley, dark jeans and a pair of black motorcycle boots, I almost forget how to breathe.

I don't think I'll ever get used to how beautifully dangerous this man looks.

He stops and his gaze locks with mine as the door closes behind him.

The intense look in his eyes is almost as if he's close to losing his shit on someone and is fighting with everything in him to keep his cool.

"Is everything okay?" I ask, my gaze slowly trailing down to see his knuckles freshly busted open. "Ace . . ."

My words trail off as he comes at me, grips the back of my head and lowers his mouth to mine.

He kisses me hard and deep, his tongue slipping between my lips with an urgency that makes my heart beat fast against my ribcage. It's almost as if he *needs* me in this moment and the idea of that has my walls crumbling even more.

"Are you off work yet?" he asks the moment our lips part.

I shake my head. "Almost. I have another twenty—"

"She's off," Gia interrupts. "Melissa can leave now if she wants."

Ace nods to Gia as he releases my head and backs away. "I'll wait outside for you."

I don't even get a chance to respond before Ace is out the door, hopping into his truck.

"Whoa," Gia whispers. "That kiss was pretty damn intense."

"Yeah." I nod and clock out, unsure of how to feel at the moment. This kiss felt *different*. So much more intense than the other ones and I know it's because my feelings for him have changed. "Thanks for letting me leave early."

"No worries. Kadence will be here soon." Her attention goes toward the window. "Enjoy your time off. I know I would if I got to stare at *him* from the passenger side of his truck." She shakes her head. "I promise I'm not thinking dirty things about your boyfriend."

"He's not my—"

"I'm pretty sure he is, Melissa. Just stay safe."

Butterflies flutter around inside my belly at the idea of Ace being my boyfriend. I like the sound of that a lot more than I ever thought I would've.

"Yeah," I whisper. "I'll see you later."

I grab my purse and head outside to Ace's truck. Just like always, he leans over and opens the door before grabbing my hand to help me up.

"Where do you want to go?" he questions, placing my hand on his firm thigh.

"I don't know." I can't think straight right now because all I can think about is why his knuckles have busted back open. "What happened to your hands?"

"Troy." He keeps his eyes on the road as he drives, his jaw steeling at the mention of this Troy guy.

"Who's Troy?"

"The fucker tied up in my garage who thought he could *hurt* my family. I'll let him go in a few days, but not until he's learned his lesson." He glances over at me and, instead of being afraid like I would've just weeks ago, I feel the urge to climb into his lap and kiss him hard on the lips.

Without giving it a second thought, I unbuckle my seatbelt and crawl into his lap, straddling him.

A deep growl comes from his throat as I kiss him hard on the lips, needing to feel his mouth on me. Needing to taste him.

I love the protective side of Ace.

"Fuck, Melissa." One of his hands moves up to wrap into the back of my hair and I feel him grow hard between my legs. "Where do you want to go? I'll take you anywhere just as long as I get to be with you."

I look up at him as he focuses on the road, his hips slightly thrusting into me as if he wants to fuck me right here in traffic. My entire body heats up at the thought.

"Take me to the garage. I want to talk and watch you work, Ace. I want to spend time with you."

He pulls up at a stoplight and moves his hands to grip my waist. "Just talking tonight," he groans. "I have somewhere I want to take you tomorrow. I *need* to because I can't control myself with you any longer." We are both breathing hard, heavy. "I want you to really see what you're getting into."

I don't know what he's talking about, but I trust him. "Okay," I whisper into his neck. "I'll go anywhere with you, Ace. But for tonight I want to just be *with* you. I missed you."

The moment the words *I missed you* leaves my lips, a small breath of relief leaves Ace's as if that's the confirmation he needed to know that I'm falling hard for him.

And I am.

I know without him saying it back that he's missed me too.

I'm not sure where he wants to take me tomorrow, but I need tonight with him. I need to get to know him before he takes me somewhere that can change *everything*.

I'm not ready to for my walls to come back up. I'm ready to fall for him completely.

15

Ace

NOT KILLING THE FUCKER IN my garage has been proving to be harder than I expected. Every time I look at the son of a bitch's face, I'm reminded of the fact that he had the power to *hurt* my family. That all it would've taken was one squeeze of the trigger for him to end my life or one of theirs.

I spent the last hour torturing him, reminding him of what will happen if he ever steps foot on our property again. The need to see Melissa in order to catch my breath and think straight was too overpowering for me not to show up at her work unexpected.

The moment my lips touched hers and her taste covered my mouth, I felt as if I could fucking breathe again.

I *need* her, and the more time we spend together, the more I know that I can't *live* without her. I don't want to.

We pull up at the garage and as usual, it's empty. Gage never stays past five because he knows I like my alone time here. My time to work and think.

Melissa is still in my lap, straddling me when I put the truck into park and it's taking every last fucking bit of my strength not to fuck her right here, right now and show her just how *mine* she truly is.

"Fuck, baby." I brush her hair back and move my lips across her ear. "I missed you, too."

My confession has her wrapping her arms around my neck and moving to place her forehead against mine. "Tell me what happened, Ace. I want to know about the asshole who got caught trying to break in. Did he hurt you?"

I shake my head and steel my jaw. "No. He almost did." I pause and run my thumb over her cheek. "If it weren't for King, though, I'd most likely be dead. He was two seconds away from pulling the trigger."

Her heart pounds angrily against my chest as her grip on me tightens. "Is there a target here?"

A small smirk crosses my face as I lift her up and out of my lap. The idea that Melissa wants to let some anger out in the same way that I've been doing for as long as I can remember somehow makes me feel even closer to her. "No, but there can be."

I watch as she jumps out of the truck and slams the door behind her. Once I make it out of the truck and over to her side, she's pacing nervously. "You could be dead right now, Ace."

She looks up, her angry gaze landing on mine as I bow my head to look down at her. "Not just me," I say on a growl. "Aston and Kadence too. Who knows what that asshole was capable of.

Still is once I free him."

She swallows hard before pulling her hair back into a ponytail. "I hate the idea of that with every fucking part of me. I want to kill that piece of shit myself."

I bring my hands up to cup her face, wanting to reassure her that he's no longer a threat. "He won't be hurting anyone after I'm through with him, Melissa. I won't fucking let him. I'd die before I let him get to you or my family. That's a promise."

Keeping her gaze on me, she nods, before reaching out to grab my hand to look at my knuckles. "I believe you, Ace."

Once we get inside, I flip on a few lights and guide Melissa into the back room that never gets used. Gabe may get upset about us leaving holes in the wall, but I'll rebuild the whole fucking wall if I have to.

I grab out my knife and hand it to Melissa before stepping back and crossing my arms. "Let it out, Angel."

She gives me a confused look. "What? Right here. Won't you get fired or–"

"I'll handle Gage," I say, cutting her off. I don't want her to think about any of that. "Don't worry about me getting into trouble."

I push away from the wall and step in close behind her, turning her to face the wall. "Pretend that piece of shit is the wall. Don't hold back." I can't lie and say I don't find pleasure in the fact she is looking out for me, that she cares enough to worry about me. Hell, it makes me really fucking happy, if I'm being honest.

She leans her head back and lets out a tiny moan when I kiss her neck. "Okay," she whispers. "I can do that."

"Good." I back away and pull the joint from my pocket as I watch her growl out and throw the knife at the wall.

A half hour goes by, and she's still not ready to give the knife back and all I can do is sit back and watch my beautiful, twisted angel with a smirk.

Fuck, how she was meant for me.

"Feel better?" I push away from the wall and walk over to the wall that has the knife stuck in it.

She nods, watching me as I pull the knife from the wall and slip it back into my boot. "I feel much better, actually."

I barely get a chance to stand back up, before her arms are wrapped around my neck and she's pulling me in for a kiss.

Fuck, how I love that she's starting to kiss me and touch me on her own. It says that we've come a long way since she first came into my life because of Aston and Kadence.

"Can I sit and watch you work now?" she questions against my lips. "It brings me peace and comfort and I need that right now."

"Yes," is all I say before guiding her back into the garage where my bike is.

I dropped it back off last night because there's still more work to get done on her.

She watches me in silence for a bit before speaking. "Were your parents ever good to you guys?" There's genuine curiosity and worry in her voice. It warms a part of my cold fucking heart.

"No," I say honestly. "Not that I can remember. I think I came out of the womb fearing them. They should've never been allowed to have kids." I look up from my bike to see her mouth curve down into a frown. "What about your parents? Are they around?"

She nods. "Yeah, they live about twenty minutes away. I see them when I can, but they both work a lot of long, crazy hours, so family time is usually few and far between." She shrugs. "We're also not real close, but we don't have any issues either. It's just sort of whatever. We make time when we can."

"They treat you well?"

"Yeah. I don't remember a time where they ever even spanked me. I guess I should be more grateful than I have been." She looks sad as her eyes move up to meet mine. "I never realized that I had it good growing up compared to some kids. I'm sorry."

"Don't be," I say stiffly. I hate thinking about my parents. "They made us who we are and I don't regret that. It also helped us get close to our uncle Killian. He's taught us a lot about life."

"I like your uncle. I can tell how much he loves you guys."

"Yeah." A grateful smile forms on my lips. "He loves us something fierce and trust me . . . Killian is the last Locke you want to cross. You think I'm twisted. Killian is brutal."

She lets out a small laugh. "I'll be sure not to get on his bad side then."

"Good. Because if you did . . . then I'd have to be on his bad side too."

She's silent as she watches me, almost as if she's unsure of what to say. I love my uncle to death, but I'd do anything for Melissa. I'm right there with her, no matter where that is.

We spend the next two hours talking, laughing and playing around and it feels incredible to be doing this with her.

I've never seen her so relaxed with me and it scares the shit out of me that after what I have to show her tomorrow, that this night, and everything that we've shared and learned about each other, might not be enough to make her want to stay.

After tomorrow, I may lose Melissa forever and, to be honest, I've never been so terrified of anything in my entire life.

That's exactly why I need to take every moment that I can get with her tonight and savor it.

After I clean off my hands, I guide Melissa out to the back of my truck and pull her into my lap, holding her as we both stare up at the night sky.

Here with her, I feel the happiest I've ever been. But for her to truly be happy with me, she needs to accept me for who I am.

Tomorrow, she'll get to see that with her own two eyes . . .

Melissa

TO SAY I AM CURIOUS about where Ace is taking me is an understatement. I glance over at him, the road we are on is rocky, as if it is foretelling me that what is about to happen, that what I am about to see would be just as uneven.

But I think this is what I need to know, whether or not falling for him completely is something I can handle.

I need to know where to go from here. Especially after the time we spent together last night. Being with him, him talking and holding me, felt so damn good to ignore.

"You don't want to tell me where we're going?" I see him smirk, but it is more of a sinister one than anything else.

Goosebumps pop out along my skin, and I know that what I

am about to witness will probably shape how I feel for Ace more than anything else that has happened since meeting him. But then again, I have a feeling that that is the reason he is taking me with him. I know that he wants me to see this other side of him, to know *truly* who he is before things get even more intense between us.

But I know about him, about his brothers and after getting to know him the way I have over the last week, I'm hoping that nothing that he can show me or tell me tonight will change how I feel for him.

Truth is, I'm already in too deep with it comes to Ace but am too afraid to actually say those words out loud. Hell, I think I'm even too afraid to admit it to myself the majority of the time.

About ten minutes later we come to a stop. There are a few houses around, all of them looking pretty rundown and deserted. Only one of them has lights coming from the inside. I glance over at Ace and see him clenching the steering wheel so tightly the leather creaks under his hold.

I want to say something, anything, but I know he's not in the mindset for anything aside from what he's about to do. And I know that's going to include violence.

He's out of the truck and reaching for his hammer before I can even comprehend it, and although I think he might say to stay in the vehicle, he walks around and opens the passenger side door.

My stomach drops, my nerves taking over.

For a second, I just sit there and stare at him, seeing the way the muscle under his jaw ticks, how he's holding the edge of the car door so tightly his knuckles are white. I can see the pulse beneath his ear beating rapidly.

He's pumped up for whatever he's about to do, or maybe he's afraid of showing me the real him. I may know what he and his brothers do, somewhat accept it now even, but witnessing it firsthand is something totally different.

I know this and it's clear he does, as well.

He helps me out of the vehicle and I stand there for a moment just staring at the house. Part of the front window is patched up with plywood, as if the owner of the house figured this was a good enough fix. The light coming from the window is dim, almost lifeless. I look over at Ace and see him watching me.

"Are you ready to see who I really am, Angel?" I open my mouth but no words come out. I want to tell him that I know who he is, but I have a feeling I really don't know who Ace Locke truly is.

"I guess I'm as ready as I'll ever be." The words fall out of my mouth, even though I'm far from ready. I spent a long time fearing the Locke brothers, not knowing who they really were, what they really stood for. I thought they were careless and dangerous. I never in my wildest dreams would've imagined I'd be where I am at this very moment.

He grins but it doesn't reach his eyes; he looks less than happy. And then together we walk up to the house. My heart is thundering and fear waves war in me. Although I know Ace would never let anything or anyone harm me, knowing I am about to see the violence that he dishes out has me on edge.

We stop right before we reach the uneven, partially broken porch steps. Headlights illuminate the house for a second, and the sound of tires on gravel ring through the air. I turn and see a dark SUV come to a stop beside Ace's vehicle. More Lockes have clearly shown up for this, and that worries me even more.

Sterling is the only one to get out, but he looks less than thrilled to see me standing there.

"What the fuck, man?" he says to Ace, but his focus is on me. "You brought your woman here? You fucking mad?"

I look at Ace and see he looks pissed off, his expression dark as he stares at Sterling. "She needs to see what we are about. She needs to know how far we go."

Sterling just shakes his head and exhales. "You're fucking insane, dude," he says under his breath. He glances at the house. "I guess if you were going to bring her with you this would be the right house to do it at. Shit that we can control."

I'm so confused at this point that I don't bother asking questions. I have to assume this is one of their "less violent" runs, because why else would Ace bring me with him if it were really dangerous?

Or maybe they are so sure of themselves that they know how this will go down before they even step foot in the house.

The latter seems more likely.

"Well," Sterling says, rolling his head around and cracking his neck. He's just as pumped up as Ace. "Let's get this fucking party started."

And just like that, my heart sinks to my stomach as the unknown presents itself.

I lift my gaze and stare at Ace's hammer, his weapon of choice. He swings it into the door, one, two, three times, before the whole thing practically comes down in front of him.

I would think seeing him with his hammer, heated and full of rage would frighten me somehow, make me think less of him, but it doesn't. In some strange way, it turns me on, knowing that he has the power to hurt some asshole who deserves it.

Ace is fearless with his hammer and I'd be lying if I said I'm not curious to see what he does with it next. I know now they don't hurt people unless it's justified and deserved. It just took me a while to realize that.

With his jaw flexed, he turns behind him and reaches for my hand. Without a word, he pulls me inside, with him leading the way.

Sterling enters behind us, and I glance at him, seeing him cross his arms over his chest and lean against the wall. He's wearing a pretty big grin. "The fucker is in the basement. I'll let you take care of the prick. I'll stay up here for backup, but I'm positive he's alone down there."

Ace grins at his brother while rolling his head around on his neck. "This piece of shit is mine and Melissa's. Just stay the fuck right there."

My heart hammers against my chest, adrenaline pumping through me as Ace grabs my hand again and begins leading me down to the basement.

Mine and Melissa's?

What does that even mean?

Why does this situation excite me, yet make me so damn nervous at the same time?

It's almost as if I want to see Ace hurt someone and I don't know how I *feel* about that.

Maybe being around Ace makes me want to be just as twisted as he is. Maybe inside, I'm just as corrupted as he is and he's been able to see it all along.

And maybe that's why I feel we are perfect for each other.

Whatever the reason, I'm about to see what Ace is all about. I'm about to see him. The *true* him.

Ace

I'VE BEEN WATCHING MELISSA SINCE the
moment we arrived. Been testing her body language, her
breathing, to see how being here makes her feel.

I'm not sure she's ready to admit it just yet, but being here,
about to hurt some motherfucker who deserves it, the excitement
of it, has her just as pumped as I am.

She's just confused by these feelings. I know this, because my
emotions were just as twisted and confusing the first time too.
Still . . . she's here with me and it doesn't look as if she plans on
running anytime soon.

The knowledge of that has me wanting to slam her against a
wall and bury myself between her thighs. Call me a sick fuck, but

the thought of catching this motherfucker, beating him until he's bloody and tying him up while I fuck *my* woman in the next room has me hard as a fucking rock.

But I school myself and gather my self-control. I can't lose focus.

This motherfucker thinks he can put his hands on a woman without her permission. Thinks he can fuck someone without their consent. But once I break both his hands and legs, let him really feel pain, he won't know the feeling of being inside a woman for a long fucking time.

I want him tortured and in agony.

Once we reach the bottom of the stairs, I turn around and back Melissa up against the wall with my body. With my free hand, I grip her neck and lean in to whisper in her ear. "Stay here." Her body is tense against mine, the anxiety practically pouring from her in waves. I close my eyes and place my hand on the center of her chest, just breathing in and out slowly, telling her, showing her without words that she's safe.

I pull back and look into her eyes. She nods in response to my statement, my demand. She's breathing a little easier now, a little more even. She looks into my eyes, her pupils dilated, her desire clear.

I smirk down at her, pleased to know that she's still turned on by me, despite the fucked-up situation I have her in right now.

With a small growl, I pull her bottom lip into my mouth, tugging it between my teeth, before I release it. "Don't move. I mean it."

"Wait," she says on a heavy breath. "I need to know what he did first. I don't know if I can stay otherwise."

I stiffen, hating the idea of saying what this sick fuck did out loud, but for her to fully understand what we do, she needs to know.

"He's a fucking rapist. A sick son of bitch who takes what he wants, when he wants. He drugs women so he can control them. The last one just happened to stay awake long enough to know it was happening."

"A rapist," she says on an angry whisper. "How many women?"

I shake my head. "Five, maybe more." I grit my teeth and grip the wood of the hammer tighter. "One was enough to punish the sick fuck and that's what I'm about to do."

She nods again, her eyes filled with anger at the knowledge of what this fucker has done. "Give him what he deserves." She looks down at my hammer as if imagining what she could do with it. "Break both of that sick asshole's legs."

I back away and swing my hammer around, my gaze still locked on hers, until I finally turn around and head for the first closed door.

The room is empty, so I move on to the only other option left down here in this creepy-ass basement.

Her words have me even more worked up, my adrenaline pumping like fucking crazy to get to this son of a bitch and hurt him.

It's almost like I'm hurting him for her now.

Bringing my boot up, I kick the door open and step inside to see a single bed and dresser set up inside the tiny room.

There's no closet and the room is fairly clean, causing me to laugh at the fact that this fucker thought he could hide from me down here.

"Trenton." I stop in front of the bed. "Are you really going to make me drag you out from under there?"

It takes a moment before I hear shuffling from under the bed. Then I see Trenton haul his ass out.

I take several steps back, curling my fingers tightly around the handle of the hammer. I can feel the smirk covering my face as the asshole stands and faces me.

He won't look me in the eye, and I can feel the fear coming from him.

Good, he needs to be afraid, because what I'm about to do to him is what nightmares are made of.

Finally, he clears his throat and shifts on his feet. He looks at me, his eyes going wide as they take in the hammer I'm holding.

He knows why I am here, and what I'm about to do.

He's heard of me. Of us Locke brothers.

Trenton holds his hands up in surrender, but that just makes me laugh. "I don't know why you're acting like this isn't going to happen." I take a step closer and he retreats one back.

"Ace-I-I swear. It was a misunderstanding."

That just pisses me off even more.

I tighten my hand even harder around the handle of the hammer and take another step closer.

The rage boils up inside of me, causing my blood to pump hard and fast through my veins. "You're actually going to stand there and tell me it was a misunderstanding?" I cock my head to the side as I appraise him. "You held her down, took from her what she wasn't willingly offering." The words come out of me like an animalistic growl. "Tell me again how innocent you are."

He is shaking his head as he retreats even farther, but the wall stops him, cornering him. I'm only a couple of feet from him now, the anger inside of me so intense I can feel it tightening my muscles, preparing me for what is about to happen.

"A misunderstanding." He says the words on a whisper, now knowing that this is going to happen no matter what.

Hell, he should have known that from the moment he knew I was here.

I am not about to prolong this. I'm going to fuck him up and then I'm going to take my woman and make her forget about tonight, about all the shitty things that she's seen, felt. I'm going to make her only feel pleasure as she stares into my eyes, knowing she's in my arms, safe and protected.

I bring my arm back, swinging my hammer forward.

I'll never let anything happen to Melissa and I'll do anything for her. She's mine, and I'm going to prove that to fucking everyone.

I connect the steel on the side of Trenton's leg, going all Misery on his ass. He screams out in pain and falls to the floor. I kick him so he moves over, and then I swing the hammer down on his other leg.

The sound of his kneecaps crushing under the onslaught of my hammer has my heart racing faster. I feel the rush of adrenaline at knowing this fucker is going to be in pain for a long time.

This fucker deserves a lot more than I'm giving him.

I swing out and knock the hammer against his knee again, then do the same to the other one. Blood is pooling through his jeans where I broke his legs, and the sight of that crimson stain spreading brings me a hell of a lot of pleasure.

I turn and stare at the door, knowing Melissa is right on the other side, no doubt hearing the screams of this piece of shit.

I wanted her here, but I didn't want her to *see* this violence, didn't want her to have that image ingrained in her memory. She needed to know exactly who I was, despite the rumors she's no doubt heard, despite the shit she knows my brothers and I do.

And tonight I gave that to her, tenfold.

Melissa

I STARE AT ACE FROM the passenger seat, watching as his broad chest quickly rises and falls.

He's focused on the road, but I catch him glancing my way every few moments as if he can't keep his eyes off me. Or maybe he's wondering how I'll react after what I heard? But I want to imagine it's the former.

I want to think that he's so drawn to me he can barely manage the simple task of driving wherever he's taking me without wanting to pull over and fuck me right here on the side of the road.

At one point I would've been nervous not knowing where he's taking me, but right now, all I feel is this overwhelming need to be alone with Ace. For him to do with me as he pleases.

As twisted as it sounds, I've been wanting him to touch me, ever since the moment he stepped out of that room and his gaze landed on mine.

There was something about the twisted smirk on his face that turned me on like nothing else.

It didn't matter to me that he'd just hurt someone and that I'd just listened to his victim screaming out in pain and begging for him to stop.

I wanted him to suffer just as badly as Ace did, and the fact that Ace was the cause of his pain only made me want him more in that moment.

Maybe I am just as fucked-up as Ace. Hell, maybe I'm more so, but as soon as I heard what that animal did, *I* wanted to hurt him my damn self. I was no longer scared of Ace's lifestyle, or what was about to go down. All I wanted was to get justice for his victims, for all the women he'd hurt in the past and was going to hurt in the future.

Ace did that. Ace did what the law wouldn't have, which was take a dangerous piece of shit off the streets for good.

The truck is filled with silence as Ace takes a quick turn onto the side road that leads to his spot in the woods.

Excitement fills me at the idea of us being here again. The memory of his hard body between my legs makes me hot and breathless.

"Does being here alone with me after what I just did make you nervous?" he asks the moment the truck comes to a stop. "Does it make you want to run now?"

I shake my head as he leans across me to undo my seatbelt.

His amber colored gaze locks with mine as he reaches his hand out and lightly squeezes my neck. It excites me more. "How about now?" His uneven breath hitting my lips has me swallowing, anticipating his next move. "Are you nervous now, Angel? Are you afraid of me?"

"No," I whisper, speaking the truth. "I wanted him to hurt. I wanted that sick son of a bitch to get what he deserved. I *wanted* you to hurt him." I lean in closer, bringing my lips close enough to brush against his. "I'm not afraid of you, Ace. I'm not going anywhere."

"Good," he growls against my lips. "I've been fucking dying to do this." He releases my neck to push the truck door open. "Don't move."

I watch as Ace jumps out of the truck. The moment he comes around to open my door and pull me down into his arms, heat fills me from the feel of his erection pressed against me.

Holding me up with one arm, he slams the truck door closed, before pressing me against it with his hard body.

"*Fuck*, Melissa. I can't control myself right now. I don't want to hurt you, but I can't be gentle. Not with how badly I *fucking* want you." The feel of his teeth scraping against my neck causes me to jump in his arms. "Tell me you can handle me or I won't touch you."

"I can more than handle you," I say honestly. I stare into his eyes when he pulls back and looks down at me. "I wouldn't want you any other way." I reach up and cup his jaw. His gaze is dark, deep, as he takes me in. "I know what I got myself into, and I'm ready for it all." I'm breathing harder, faster, unable to keep myself under control either. "I've been waiting for this for a long time, Ace."

He makes this deep growl, this animalistic sound that has chills racing along my body.

"I want you here, Ace. I want you now." I don't want a bed, don't want romantic or sweet and gentle.

I knew what I was getting into when I fell hard for Ace. There's no going back, but I wouldn't have wanted to anyway.

Before I know what is happening, or can prepare myself, Ace is leading me toward the back of the truck, pulling the blanket he has on the bed flush, and helps me up so I'm sitting in the tailgate. He sits beside me and pulls me onto his lap, my legs spread on either side of him, my chest pressed to his.

His hands are on my lower back, his fingers digging into the skin that is exposed because my shirt rode up. We are staring at each other, neither speaking, but nothing needs to be said. The magnetism I feel is tangible, like fingers skating over my body.

Then he slides one hand up my back, tangles his fingers around my hair, and tugs on the strands until my head cocks back and I gasp from the pain. But on the heels of that, this pleasure washes through me, making me wet, needy.

"You sure you want to go here with me?" he asks in a deep, guttural voice, one that is like a serrated knife moving over my body.

I get wetter.

I nod. "I want this." I am so ready for him. "I've wanted this for a while, Ace, but was too afraid to say anything, to act on it."

"And you're not afraid now?"

I shake my head slowly. I don't need to think about what he said, but I stay silent for a few seconds. "I'm not afraid of you, but of how I feel."

He seems to dig his fingers into me harder, as if he doesn't want to let me go. "And how do you feel, baby?"

My throat is tight, my mouth dry. I don't know if admitting this to him is the best course, but I also know I can't hide how I feel. I can't pretend anymore. I won't. "I want you so bad that it hurts."

And then he has his mouth on mine, his tongue speared between my lips. Ace kisses me brutally, violently almost, but I love it. I want more of it, so much more that I'm drowning in it. We are both panting, gasping for breath when he pulls away a moment later.

"I won't fuck you in the back of my truck, not when I need you on my bed, surrounded by my things, smelling like me."

I'm about to tell him I don't care where we do this, because I need him too desperately. But before I can get a word out he's helping me off the truck, back into the passenger side seat, and is driving, presumably to his house. It all happens so fast I am dizzy from it all, can't even take enough air into my lungs.

This is really going to happen, and I'm not going to stop it.

I feel like we are back at the Locke house faster than normal, but then again, I think Ace was driving well above the speed limit. It seems he's just as frantic to start this as I am. I glance down and see the massive erection straining against his pants. He is ready for me, just as much as I am, my panties soaked, my nipples hard. Every part of me is screaming to finally be with Ace, to let him claim me, own every inch of me.

We stare at each other for long seconds, the heat and air in the truck getting thicker, hotter. I want to just have him take me right here, right now. I don't care if anyone sees us.

In fact, this part of me wants it to be known that I'm claimed by Ace, that I am with a Locke. I want anyone who looks at me to know that if they fuck with me they'll get wrath tenfold in return.

"I hope you're really ready for this, Melissa."

I swallow, the lump in my throat thick. "I've been ready," I say again, meaning it more than I ever have.

I don't wait for him to help me out of the truck this time. I get out and meet him at the hood of the vehicle. He growls low, and I know it's because he wants to be in charge, to call the shots. I am more than okay with that.

I can feel my heart pounding in my chest, and I wonder if he can hear it, see it beating at the pulse point below my ear. He takes my hand and leads me inside, up the stairs, and finally into his room. Once the door is shut, we stand there in silence, this thickness coating both of us, drawing us together.

"Take off your clothes for me," he demands in a low, deep voice, one that lets me know this isn't going to be slow and gentle. I already knew that, but it's another affirmation of who I am with.

And then I'm removing my clothes, feeling like Ace is the predator and I'm his prey.

That analogy can't be further from the truth.

I know that after tonight there really is no going back. But then again, I am already Ace's.

I have been since the moment I saw him. I just didn't know it yet . . .

19

Ace

MY COCK HARDENS EVEN MORE as I stand back and watch Melissa undress herself. Fuck, how it hurts to not be inside her right now, taking her hard and rough against every surface in this room.

She moves slow, almost as if to tease me, and it's driving me fucking mad, twisting me up until I feel as if I'm about to explode.

I can't handle the wait any longer.

Closing the distance between us, I press my body against hers as I back her to the wall and brush my lips against her smooth neck. "I need it all off," I growl. "I need you naked, Angel."

She lets out a small gasp as I move my mouth around to the front of her neck and gently dig my teeth in before licking her skin where I just bit her. "You're *mine*, Melissa. After tonight, no other man will get to kiss you . . ." I move my lips up to brush over hers. "To taste you. And honestly, after knowing you've been with *me*, no other man will want to come near you for fear of me breaking their fucking legs and arms. This is it."

I hear her swallow before she lets out a soft "I'm ready," across my lips, confirming what I already knew from the first moment we kissed. She's already mine.

As soon as the words leave her mouth, my hands are gripping her waist and flipping her around to press her front against the wall. The feel of her round ass against my hard cock has me moaning and biting my bottom lip with need.

She's about to be *fucked* by the most dangerous Locke brother of us all, when in the beginning, she feared us and wanted *nothing* to do with us.

Fuck, how that turns me on.

I move my hands down her body, slow at first, but the moment I reach the top of her thong, I rip the thin material down her legs and slam my body against hers, unable to be gentle with her.

"Take your jeans off, Ace." She sounds needy as she grips at the wall, taking heavy breaths. "I need you inside me. *Now.*"

Pressing her harder into the wall with my hips, I undo her bra, pulling the straps down her arms before grazing my teeth over her neck, right over the pulse that throbs beneath her ear. My cock jerks.

With a deep growl, I reach between our bodies and undo my jeans, sliding them down enough to pull my hard cock out and slide it against her ass.

I take my hand and slap her ass a few times, causing her to throw her head back and moan out, my cock now so fucking close to her needy pussy. The sound of her moans has me close to coming all over her ass, before I can even get inside of her.

I position myself at her pussy, feeling how hot and wet she is, how tight and mine she is. I lean in and growl into her ear, "Hold on tight, Angel."

With that, I slam into her.

I do it so fucking hard that she turns her head and bites into my arm, cussing from the intrusion of me stretching her pretty little pussy.

Groaning against the back of her neck, I wrap my fingers into her long hair and pull as I use my other hand and reach around to grip her throat, pulling her back so I can graze my teeth along the side of her neck.

My thick cock fills her, taking her deep and hard, her wetness coating me as I claim her as mine.

Something in me snaps and I start thrusting back and forth, shoving my big, thick cock deep in her wet, hot pussy. She's wet, so damn wet that the juicy sounds of me fucking her fill my head, echoing off the walls. I'm grunting like a damn animal, but I can't help it. I'm finally claiming Melissa as mine, and there's no going back.

I have my hands on her hips, my fingers digging into her sides. I know there will be bruises in the morning, but I like that. I want my mark on her, want anyone who sees her to know who she belongs to. And she belongs to me, the same way I belong to her.

I push into her and pull out several more times, both of us moaning, sweat covering our bodies. I could fuck her against the wall all night long, but I want her on my bed, covered in my scent.

I force myself to pull out of her, both of us groaning in disappointment. I have her turned around and on my bed in seconds flat. She's breathing hard, fast, her breasts shaking slightly, her nipples pink and hard, the tips making my mouth water. I reach down and grab my cock, stroking myself from root to tip, about to come just from the look of her.

Her legs are slightly spread, her pussy bare of any hair. I love that she shaves, love that I can see how pink and glossy she is, how primed I've made her. I start jerking off faster and harder, wishing my cock was in her pussy again, but I'm too aroused to even move. My dick is slightly slick from being buried deep inside of her, and I need that hot wetness coating me again.

I'm on her before I can even think, this primal instinct taking over. I force her legs apart with my hands on her inner thighs, this small gasp leaving her. I align myself at her pussy again, staring right into her eyes as I thrust in deep and hard.

The force of my action has her moving up the bed. She closes her eyes, tips her head back, and opens her mouth on this silent cry. I move my hands up to her waist, digging my fingertips into her again. And then I really fuck her.

In and out.

Faster and harder.

I'm growling like a madman, unable to stop myself. I'm holding off from coming because I want this to last, because I want to feel her cunt squeezing me as she climaxes.

"Come for me, squeeze me, Melissa. Get the cum out of me." Fuck, I'm a dirty bastard. And then she cries out and obeys so damn nicely. I feel her pussy clenching around my dick, drawing my seed from my balls. I can't hold off, not when she feels so damn good.

She cries out and I groan, my cock feeling like it's getting strangled. I'm not going to be able to hold out. I don't want to. I pull out and push back in. Pull out and push back in. On the third thrust I bury myself completely in her, my balls slapping her ass, my orgasm rushing up.

I fill her with my seed, make her take it all. The pleasure is intense, consuming. Only when I feel the ecstasy start to wane do I pull back, slipping from her tight pussy for a moment. I keep her legs spread open with my hands as I stare at where I was just buried. And then I see my cum start to slip from her body.

I slip back inside of her, keeping my seed where it belongs. I look at her face, seeing her drowsy, post-euphoric expression and feel possessive and territorial.

"You are mine."

Melissa

I CAN BARELY CATCH MY breath from the way Ace fucked me just now. I thought I was ready. That I'd be able to handle his rough possessiveness in the bedroom, but truthfully, I'll be surprised if I can walk out of here after the way he just claimed me.

How will I be able to do that when I can barely even move because my legs are shaking so damn hard below his body?

"Are you okay, Angel?" His muscles flex above me as he lowers his soft mouth to hover over my mine. "This . . . the way I just *fucked* you was me holding back. It's too soon for me to give it to you like I fucking crave to. You're not ready for *me* yet."

"What if I am?" I ask on a whisper, closing my eyes as his

tongue flicks out to run across my lips. "I'm ready for all of you, Ace."

He lets out this deep, throaty laugh and grips my chin, pulling it up so our eyes meet. With his gaze locked on mine, he pulls my bottom lip between his teeth, causing me to let out a small cry as he bites me. Hard. So hard that it draws blood.

Then he takes his tongue and moves it across the wound as if to ease the pain he just caused. "Not yet."

I lay back and stare at him as he watches me for a moment. He's yet to pull out of me and the thought of his cum inside of me, filling me, has me remembering a really important fact.

"You never asked me if I was on birth control," I point out, feeling a bit anxious over just having unprotected sex. I should be freaking out more, but something in me is holding that down, telling me everything will be fine.

"Because I don't care if you are or not. I was going to fill you with my cum either way." His breath hits my lips as he speaks and for some strange reason, the fact that he came in me without asking has me completely turned on. "You're mine," he whispers against my lips, while moving his fingers down in between our bodies, possessively. "It's been a very long time since I was with a woman and I've always used protection . . . up until now. You're different, special. I want your pussy filled with my seed every fucking night, Angel."

With a growl, he pulls out of me and spreads my legs apart, bringing his hands up to grip my thighs. His lips curve into a satisfied grin as he looks down, no doubt seeing his cum slipping out of my pussy. "So fucking perfect."

After a second of just staring at me, he stands up and reaches for his shirt to wipe me off with. My heart races in my chest as I watch him clean me off and toss the shirt aside.

His naked body is pure perfection as he stands before me and it's hard for me to pull my gaze away, but I manage to long enough for me to crawl out of bed and get dressed, too.

When I turn back around, he's standing there, naked, with a cigarette hanging between his lips as he watches me.

"I should get going now."

He doesn't say anything. He just lights up his smoke and opens the window, before walking over to lock his bedroom door.

He doesn't have to say anything. I know he's telling me to stay, and to be honest I want the same thing.

Ace

I DON'T WANT MELISSA TO go. Ever. Although I'm not a dumb fuck, and I know she can't be by my side at all times, the possessive fucker in me wants her locked in my room.

I sit in a chair in the corner and watch Melissa sleep. The soft rise and fall of her stomach underneath a thin sheet. The sheet has fallen just below her breasts, and my focus is trained on the perfect mounds, the fact her nipples are hard, the cool air kissing them. She is perfect.

She is mine.

She might have been afraid of the person I am, the things I do. But she is strong. She came with me, saw me in action, well, as much as I'd allow her to see. I didn't want her witnessing the gruesome and violent things I did even if it was the life the Lockes led.

I also don't want to hide who I am from her. And the fact she hasn't run screaming tells me she is perfect for me. I was right about that from the beginning.

I stand up and leave my room, shutting the door softly behind me. I know she's going to be hungry when she wakes up, so I head down to the kitchen to make us some food.

I see Sterling at the table, a half-eaten plate pushed aside, his foot kicked up on the edge of a chair. He's shirtless, with his jeans unbuttoned and unzipped, and his hair a wild fucking mess. The asshole doesn't even live here anymore, but him and Wynter still stay here some nights.

Looks like I'm not the only one who claimed my woman last night. He gives me a funny look and I grin, shaking my head, telling him without words to not even ask. What I share with Melissa is pretty fucking private. Even though I love my brothers and would die for them, kill for them, talking about being with Melissa is not something I want to do.

Which to be honest is pretty damn strange, given the fact I don't hide anything from Aston or Sterling.

"Looks like you had a long night," Sterling says, amusement in his voice.

I look over at my brother and scowl. "I could say the same thing to you." I laugh. "Looks like you've been ridden hard and put away wet." Sterling snorts and runs a hand over his face.

"Dude," he shakes his head. "I'm not even going go into my relationship with Wynter, but I can see you're right there with me where Melissa is concerned." Sterling grins. "And it's about damn time you fell hard."

And then Aston comes in, the third Locke looking worse than either of us. Sterling and I both start laughing, knowing that all of us are good and fucked where our women are concerned.

Aston stops and stares at us, his brows furrowed. "You guys look like shit, like you got no fucking sleep last night."

I look at Sterling and we both start laughing harder.

Hell, all of us are sure as fuck something to look at now. Yeah, I did fall pretty fucking hard. But hell, I'd bring down the whole damn world if it meant Melissa was happy.

I grab some food and go back upstairs, head into my room and shut the door softly. I set the food aside, get undressed, and slip under the covers beside Melissa. She smells so damn good, and her body is so soft, so warm. I feel her stirring beside me, and she shifts, turning over so she's looking at me now, this sleepy expression on her face.

I don't say anything, just cup her face and lean in, kissing her softly. After long seconds we're both breathing hard. My cock is stiff as fuck, pressing against her belly, needing to be inside of her. I roll her over so she's now on her back. I am on top of her, using my knee to spread her thighs, fitting my body between them, my cock running between her folds.

I kiss her again, reach between our bodies, and align myself at her pussy. And then I thrust in nice and slow. I'm not fucking her right now, even though I want to go fast and hard, be raw and rough. I take my time, pushing in and pulling out, driving her higher, making things hotter.

She's so fucking wet for me, and the soft mewls she makes has me becoming frenzied. But I go slow, make this sweet and gentle. This might be the only time I am like this, but right now this is how it has to be.

Right now this is what I want with Melissa. She's mine, every part of her, and I want to take my time, savor every moment I have with her.

Because after this moment there won't be any more making love. There will just be hardcore claiming my woman.

Melissa

I GOT OFF WORK AN hour ago, but came home first to change for the bonfire that's at Ace's house tonight. The fact I'll get to see him, maybe even make what we have official in some capacity, makes my heart speed up. I'm done hiding, pretending like I am too afraid of my own feelings to let them be known. I want the whole damn world to know that Ace is mine and I'm his.

I've slept the last two nights at his place and have only been home for twenty minutes at a time, just long enough to grab clean clothes to change into before I head back to see him. He makes me feel whole, like the person I truly am has been dormant this whole time, just waiting for him to spark it to life.

This is the first time that I've been here for longer and it feels weird all of a sudden, like I'm in someone else's place, as if this is no longer mine and Kadence's home. A part of me feels a bit sad about that, simply because this has been my "safe place" for a while now, where I felt sheltered and safe.

But I feel that way with Ace, and no matter where I am, as long as he's there I'm golden.

I grab the rest of my stuff and head out to my car. After tossing the bag in the backseat I climb behind the wheel, crank the engine, and turn on the radio. I drive around for a bit, wanting to take a moment to drive by mine and Kadence's old place. Once I arrive outside I can't help but look at the house across the street. It all started there, seemingly ages ago.

That's when I first came in contact with the Locke brothers, when they weren't just rumors to me. It's then that I should have known I was in deep, that I couldn't just ignore this . . . that I'd be swept under in the best of ways. When I saw Kadence with Aston I felt like she was living for the first time. I never told her, but I'd been jealous of her, envious of the kind of fire I saw between the two of them.

I have that now, though. I have it for myself.

I finally arrive at the Locke property and already see a blazing bonfire lit up. There are chairs around the fire pit, and I immediately notice Sterling and Wynter, Aston and Kadence sitting around. I even see the Locke brothers' Uncle Killian standing off to the side, a beer in his hand.

I park the car and cut the engine. As soon as I'm out I see Ace striding over, a grin on his face. My heart jumps to my throat. It seems whenever he's around I get this instant reaction, like I haven't seen him in years. Part of me knows that this won't ever change, that it will always be like this between us.

He wraps his arms around me and pulls me close to his chest.

He has his hand on my nape, tips my head to the side, and slams his mouth on mine. I can't help but moan at the flavor of him as he strokes the seam of my lips with his tongue.

When he pulls away I'm left breathless, wanting more, craving it. I look over at the bonfire and can see the brothers and their women looking at us, each one wearing a smile. I feel my face heat. Although this is what I wanted. I want them to know I'm with Ace. Hell, I need everyone to know that he's mine in the same way he wants them to know I'm his.

We're not that different.

We walk over to the fire and he sits down, immediately pulling me onto his lap and holding me close. It feels good being on his lap, his arms around me, everyone staring at us. I don't feel weird that we have all this attention. It's what I want, what I need.

I turn and look at Ace, and feeling my emotions rise up, I'm the one who kisses him this time. I press my tongue to his lips, stroking so he opens for me, and then I delve inside. I'm normally not so wanton or brazen. I like when Ace takes control, has the power. But I want him to see, to feel that I'm right here with him, that I want him as much as he wants me.

I hear Sterling whistle under his breath, can hear Aston saying something to Kadence about the PDA between Ace and I, but I don't care. I'm focused on the man I love.

I love him.

He groans but pulls away, and I'm left there panting, wanting more. Needing it.

"If we don't stop I'll have you in my room in my bed."

I smile. "Maybe that's what I want."

He groans again and rests his forehead on mine.

"You're just as fucking insatiable as I am."

I chuckle.

But I face the fire, knowing that being here with Ace, without us being naked, is just as good as when we are alone in his room. It might be better, if I am being honest.

For long moments he just holds me, and I listen to the brothers bullshit, even hear Killian telling a story or two about all the shit he used to get into when he was their ages. There are laughs, a lot of touching from the guys and their women, and for the first time in a long damn time I feel like I belong someplace.

Like I really belong here.

These guys are family, and I am now part of that circle. But this has me thinking about what and who Ace is, and more specifically, whom he has in the garage. I twist slightly and look at said building, knowing who is behind those double doors, who has crossed a Locke.

"Ace?" I ask softly and face him again, looking into his eyes.

"Yeah, baby." He lifts his hand and smooths his thumb over my bottom lip.

"Show me him." I know I don't have to elaborate on who I'm talking about. I see the way Ace's expression changes, how he becomes tense beneath me.

"You want to see him?"

I nod and lick my lips. "I need to see him." And I realize I've never spoken truer words. In this moment I realize I am not so different than the man I love.

22

Ace

I PAUSE OUTSIDE THE GARAGE door and stare for a few moments, feeling somewhat anxious that Melissa wants to see this fucker.

She's *heard* the damage I do, has heard the breaking of bones and the screams of my victim, but her *seeing* the damage is something else entirely.

We're just now beginning to feel like a real couple. Her walls are no longer up when she's with me and the thought that once she sees with her own two eyes the damage I've done to this prick, that she might pull back from *us,* has me feeling on edge.

"I'm ready, Ace." She gives my hand a slight squeeze as if to reassure me that she's ready to witness this mangled prick.

Ever since I mentioned to her what this fucker did, that he almost killed me, I can tell that she's been wanting to see the person who was almost responsible for taking me away from her.

There's anger in her eyes and in her voice every time I mention that I'm going out to the garage, but I've made it a point to keep her away from him.

"Once you see what I've done, you can't *unsee* that shit, Melissa." I turn and grab her chin, pulling it up so our gazes meet. "I need to know for sure that you're ready for that. I can't fucking lose you now that you're mine. I won't."

She keeps her gaze locked on mine, a softness in them as if wanting to show me that she's not going anywhere. "You'll never lose me, Ace. Nothing you can do can scare me away now that I know the *real* you." Her hands move up to grip my shirt as she stands on the tips of her toes and brushes her lips against mine. "I'm not going anywhere. Now show me."

I swallow nervously before grabbing the back of her head and kissing her. She kisses me back with a roughness that has me growling against her lips with need.

"Fuck, Angel," I whisper as we break the kiss. "I'm getting really fucking close to taking you upstairs and claiming you instead."

Her gaze lowers to my dick as I reach down to adjust my erection. A twisted smile crosses her face as she steps in close and runs her hand down my body. "You can claim me after. Like I said . . . I'm not going anywhere."

Before I can lose all self-control and throw her over my shoulder, carry her upstairs and fuck her like the twisted fucker that I am, I release my grip on her head and make my way over to the garage door to open it.

I step inside first, Melissa following right behind me, so close that I can feel the warmth from her body against my backside.

Troy is still hanging there all bloodied, cut up and bruised just as I've left him every night since he showed up on our property.

He's lucky I've been *kind* enough to provide him with water and food to keep his ass alive. Honestly, I could care less if he starves to death out here, but not getting the chance to hurt him and make him suffer for what he *almost* did is what I can and do care about.

He begins thrashing around at the sight of me, and although there's no way in hell he can get to Melissa to hurt her, I find myself pushing her behind me and growling out in anger.

"Keep fucking moving and I'll have to break all the fingers on your other hand too." The tilt of my head as I stare across the garage at him has him obeying me. He's learned enough over the time since he's been my prisoner what that look means.

I feel Melissa move around me, finally stepping out from behind me to get a look at Troy.

She stands frozen for a few moments, staring up at him as if to take all the damage in.

All I can do is watch her as she watches him, wanting to see every single one of her facial expressions.

At first she looks a little shocked by all the cuts and broken bones, but then her expression changes into anger and determination as if she wants to make him suffer at her hands too.

"He almost killed you," she whispers. "He almost took you from me and possibly even Kadence if he had the chance."

I nod as she turns her attention to me. "Yes."

I watch closely as she walks over to stand in front of me, before kneeling down to reach into my boot for the knife she knows I keep hidden there. The one she's used on more than one occasion to let out some frustration.

She stands and grips the knife, her head tilting to the side as she looks down at it. In this moment, she reminds me a lot of myself. I can almost *feel* her need to hurt him, to cause damage because of the damage he could've and would've caused had he had the chance.

"He hasn't suffered enough yet," she says softly, looking up at me. "I want him to know that if he *ever* hurts anyone that I love that I will hurt him far worse. He needs to know never to come back here again."

I steel my jaw and watch as she turns around and throws the knife at Troy, the blade sticking right into his thigh.

She's breathing heavily, standing still as she watches him.

I feel joy as he screams out in pain and begins thrashing around again. But joy isn't the only thing I feel at the fact that my girl is the one hurting this piece of shit. I feel relief and peacefulness, knowing that Melissa isn't going anywhere.

This moment right here is the confirmation I needed to know Melissa is truly mine for good.

She's not going anywhere.

I don't only want her in this moment, but I *need* her.

It looks like she's about to walk over to grab the knife out of Troy, possibly to hurt him again, but I grab her by the hips and flip her around so that she's facing me.

We're both breathing heavily as I look down at her. My need to have her, to claim her in this very moment, has me gripping onto her body so hard that my fingers hurt. I've never needed to take Melissa as rough and wild as I do right this fucking second.

She doesn't need *gentle*.

She doesn't *want* gentle.

She fucking needs *me*.

With a growl, I pick her up and carry her outside and to the side of the garage where I know no one will bother looking for us. Shit, even if they did, I'm not sure I'd give a fuck at the moment.

The craving to be inside my woman is too strong.

I can see the need in her eyes too . . . can feel her desire from the rapid beating of her chest against mine as she looks up at me. It has me feeling like a fucking animal ready to strike. With a groan, I set her down just long enough to rip her jeans and panties down her legs and free my cock from my pants. Then I pick her back up, align my erection with her pussy and slam into her so hard that she screams out and digs into my skin, drawing blood.

With each hard thrust of my hips, I push her body up the side of the garage, causing her to scream louder and tear at my flesh as if she's feeling just as wild and animalistic as I am.

"God . . . Ace . . ." she pants against my lips, her nails digging in further. The feel of her leaving marks has me going even harder. "Keep going . . . keep going . . ."

I thrust into her again and stop, leaning my head back as she pulls on my hair.

"Fuck . . ." I growl into the night sky, loving the way she's being rough with me. Her roughness is fueling me to fuck her harder . . . and harder . . . taking her with every bit of strength that I have without breaking her in two.

I can barely fucking breathe. Both of our bodies are dripping with sweat, but I keep going, giving us both what we want.

Wild, untamed sex.

With the way she's handling me, I'll be covered with bruises and scratches by the time I come inside of her, and of course that shit only turns me on more. I want my woman to hurt me. I want her to do with me as she fucking pleases, because it shows me that she's claiming me as I've claimed her.

My beautiful, twisted angel.

We were meant for each other, in every fucking way.

Being inside of her has me so fucking heated that I end up

biting into her lip and drawing blood. When she moans out in plea-sure from it, I feel a tug at my balls, fucking ready to bust inside her. "Come for me, Angel," I growl against her mouth. "Right. Now."

Within seconds, her pussy squeezes my dick, drawing the cum straight from my cock. I push in as far as I can and fill her with my seed again, loving that Melissa is the first one to have *all* of me.

Every twisted part of me belongs to her.

I love her, and I'd kill and die for her without a second thought.

This woman, right here in my arms, is mine and I'll do every-thing in my power to keep it that way.

She sags against me and for long seconds we stand here, pant-ing, breathing each other's air, being in the same headset as the other. I knew the moment I'd seen her that she was mine, that I'd do whatever in my power I could to ensure that. It took a long time, too damn long for Melissa to be claimed by me, but I have her now. That's all that matters. They'll have to cut out my beating heart for me to let her go.

They can try, but they won't succeed. Because when you've got something so good nothing else matters, you'll lay bodies at your feet to ensure you never let it go.

That's what I have with Melissa.

The ground I walk on will be littered with the fallen who try to take her from me.

EPILOGUE

Melissa

Six months later

I STARE AT THE BOXES that litter my living room. Anything that means something to me is packed away, ready to be housed in a new location, a new home. Hell, *I'm* about to go to a new place without Kadence.

I'm about to *live* with Ace.

I can't say that I'm not scared, that the anxiety of something new doesn't terrify me. But I'm going to be with Ace, and that's all that matters. I decided that it's the right time to move in together, and although he asked me a month ago, and at first I said I didn't know, it hasn't taken me long to realize this is exactly what I want.

He's exactly what I want in my life.

Forever.

The thought of not being with him . . . of not touching, kissing or holding him *kills* me. My feelings for him have only grown stronger with each day.

Ace, Sterling, and Aston all come in through the front door to grab some more boxes. They brought their vehicles, packing them full of my stuff. This has been my home for over a year now, one I shared with Kadence. But she and Aston are going to live together now, Wynter is with Sterling, and I'm finally with the man that I love.

I look over at him and can't help the way my heart starts beating faster. It's an instant reaction when I'm near him.

Sterling and Aston grab a few more boxes and head out just as Kadence and Wynter walk in. The whole family has been helping, and I can't help but feel like that's truly what they are . . . my family.

Ace pulls me in for an embrace before I even know he's right in front of me. I rest my head on his chest, inhaling deeply, taking in the woodsy, purely masculine scent of him.

"You sure about this?" he asks in his gruff voice.

"More than I've ever been about anything else." I pull back and look at him, smiling as I stare into his face. This is exactly what I'm supposed to do, where I'm supposed to be. After all the shit I've been through with Ace, all the things I've seen, participated in, I know that I was always meant to be with him.

The rumors, the fear I felt when I heard about the Locke Brothers, before I even knew Ace, knew any of them, are distant memories now. These men protect what they hold dear, and to Ace I am his world.

He cups my cheek and leans down to kiss me soundly on the lips. "I love you, baby. So fucking much."

Hearing Ace say those words, knowing that for as hardcore and rough he is, that to him I am everything, takes the breath straight from my lungs. "I love you, too."

He grins and kisses me again. "You ready to live with the most twisted Locke of all? I'll promise no more prisoners in the garage . . . for a while at least."

"I can work with that." I grin against his mouth when he growls, most likely wanting an answer from me. "And yes. I've been ready for a while now. It just took some time to realize that. There's nowhere else I'd rather be, Ace."

There's no other man or person for that matter that could ever make me feel the way that Ace does.

The excitement.

The feeling of being alive . . . living on the edge.

The overwhelming feeling of need whenever he's present.

And most of all . . . the safety and security I feel whenever I'm wrapped up in his strong arms, feeling his heartbeat, is perfection.

Ace is it for me.

He's the one and there's nothing in this world that could ever make me give him up.

I am his world and he is *mine*.

Ace

THE FACT THAT MY BROTHERS and I moved Melissa's things into the Locke house has me feeling like the happiest man on earth.

It took a month for me to convince her to say yes, but I knew she'd eventually want the same as me. That she'd want to fall asleep next to me and wake up beside me every day of the fucking week.

That's what I want.

It's not as if she hasn't been doing that, but it wasn't her waking up in *our* bed or in *our* house and the idea of that has been eating at me deep.

Ever since Melissa and I made things official, Aston and Kadence have been spending most of their time at Kadence's, so it just made sense that Aston and Kadence would live there, and Melissa would move into the Locke house with me.

We're all close and able to have each other's backs and that's what's most important.

All except for Uncle Killian.

Last I heard, he was in a different town busting faces and being the most brutal Locke of us all.

He'll be back eventually. He always is.

He never was one to stay in this town for too long.

I look over and smile at the sight of Melissa pulling the blanket from the back of the couch and wrapping it around her, getting comfortable.

She's been living here for less than twenty minutes and she's already treating my home as hers.

Our home.

Good. That fucking makes me happy.

"Come here, baby." I pull her into my lap and wrap us both up with the blanket. She smiles against my lips, showing me she's just as happy about living here as I am that she is.

"I can't believe that I'm living in the Locke house." She grabs my hand and moves it over her belly. "That this will be *our* home."

My eyes widen as I look down at her stomach. "Fuck, baby. Please tell me that–"

"I'm pregnant," she says, cutting me off with excitement. "We're having a baby."

Hearing her say that she's carrying my child has my heart filling with a happiness I've never felt before. Hell, I never thought this would happen to me, that I'd even find a woman to have by my side, let alone be a father. But if I'm going to do it I sure as hell want to do it with Melissa.

Yes, Melissa makes me happy. She makes me more than happy, but this feels *different*.

She's having *my* baby.

"Hell yeah!" I roar out with excitement before I set her on her feet and drop down to my knees in front of her. My entire body is shaking as I grab her hips and move in to kiss her belly. "I fucking love you and I promise you with everything I am that I will love our baby and protect it always."

She grabs my face and pulls it up until I'm looking at her as she looks down at me. "I believe it with my whole heart. No one loves or protects fiercer than you do."

I grin up at her. She's my world, and the child she carries brings this whole situation full circle. I may be one twisted as fuck Locke, but hell, when it comes to Melissa, to our baby, I'm not very tough at all.

There's nothing better than knowing you've got it good, even if maybe you don't deserve it.

"What's all the fucking excitement in here?" Sterling sticks his head through the doorway and checks me out on my knees, while holding a burger in his hand. "Why are you on . . . oh fuck."

I nod and stand to my feet before grabbing Melissa's face and kissing her hard. I want to show my brother just how happy I am. "Oh fuck is right. I'm going to be a dad and I'm happy as shit about it. Call the others in here. Now."

Sterling's face turns up into a proud smile. "Shit . . . I'm going to be an uncle." Ignoring my orders, he comes at Melissa and kisses her hard on the top of the head. "That's going to be one lucky kid. Us Lockes always look out for each other. *You're* a Locke now too, sister."

I smile at the happiness filling Melissa's eyes. "Thank you,

Sterling. Now go get the others."

"Yes, ma'am. You, I'll take orders from." Sterling flips me the middle finger and takes off.

That dick. He's lucky he listens to my woman at least.

I can barely keep my hands off Melissa's stomach while waiting for everyone else to join us in the living room.

I feel as if I'm about to fucking burst with happiness and pride.

Kadence is the first to join us, followed by Wynter and then Aston, who crosses his arms and leans against the wall.

"This better be good. Kadence and I were *busy*." He spins his lock around his finger, while looking over at me.

"Shut up, asshole. I don't want you ruining our moment."

"I'm just going to say it," Melissa says with excitement. "Ace and I are having a baby. You're all going to be aunts and uncles."

Kadence is the first to react. She runs at Melissa and throws her arms around her. "I'm so happy for you guys. I knew it. I *knew* you and Ace would end up together. You have no idea how happy I am for you."

I look over to see Aston finally push away from the wall. His lips curve up into a smile as he tosses his lock aside and walks over to pick Melissa up and kiss her on the lips.

"Hey, asshole. Don't make me cut those bitches off."

Before I can get too upset with Aston for kissing my woman, Kadence laughs and punches him on the arm while we watch Wynter attack Melissa with a hug.

Everyone is surrounding us now, everyone happier than I've ever seen them, and I know without a doubt that our baby will be happy and loved.

We're a family.

We're the Lockes.

We play hard, destroy even harder, but most of all . . . we love with everything in us . . .

THE END

Continue on to read the first three chapters of STRUNG by Victoria Ashley.

Excerpt from *Strung* by Victoria Ashley

Chapter One

Tegan
Arlington, Wisconsin

WHEN MY PHONE DECIDES TO vibrate across the bedside table for a fourth time within two minutes, I roll over and scowl at it, seriously considering breaking the darn thing against the wall.

I can barely even keep my eyes open this early in the morning, let alone manage to muster up the energy to reach over and read any stupid messages.

I wish my phone would get the damn memo, but apparently it doesn't, because it vibrates for a fifth time.

Annoyed, I growl out and reach for it.

There's only *one* person crazy enough to bother me this early in the morning.

One person, and that jerk is lucky he happens to be my brother. If I didn't love him so much I'd kill him. Especially since he *knows* how much my sleep means to me.

Alexander Tyler . . . I will break your pretty face!

I don't even bother reading his five messages before replying with an angry response. It's too early for me to give a damn right now.

After the party my friends threw for me last night, I needed every second of sleep I could get this morning to recover from my hangover, and he just ruined that for me.

My head hurts like hell and a wave of nausea hits as I press the send button.

Me: Piss off, Xan! I'm sleeping. STOP texting me!

Xan: Morning, Sunshine. And what the fuck did I tell you about calling me Xan?

Me: You told me not to do it. Now what the hell do you want, Xan?

I grunt as I look over at my alarm clock to see it's only ten past five. I want to reach through the phone and choke his annoying butt even more now.

With the way *every* little *part* of my body aches, I knew it was early, but I didn't realize it was the ass-crack of dawn.

"He is so fucking unreal," I grunt, while reading his next message as it pops up.

Xan: If you would read my messages then you would know why the hell I'm texting and we wouldn't be having this conversation. Scroll up, genius.

Trying my best to focus on the blurred words, I run my hand over my face and scroll up to the first message, before quickly replying.

I should've known.

That bar is his damn life now. I'm not sure anything else matters to him more than *Vortex*.

> Me: *Seriously? You won't be home when I arrive? You have a serious work problem, Xan. You couldn't even take the day off for your little sister's arrival?*

> Xan: *Go back to sleep. You shouldn't be awake so damn early anyway. You don't have to be at the airport for another three hours.*

> Me: *Asshole! It's your fault I'm awake. So how am I getting into the house?*

> Xan: *The back. In the rock by the sliding door. See you tonight, baby sis. Oh . . . and enter the house with caution.*

> Me: *Yeah . . . sure. Thanks for the warning. NOW BYE.*

"Ugh!"

After I toss my phone aside, I close my eyes and try to force myself back to sleep, but all I can think about is the fact that in less than nine hours I'll be in California, chilling by the ocean and working on my new book, away from this small town and my overbearing parents.

My brother left as soon as he turned twenty-one and I've been waiting very *impatiently* to do the same. It's the only request that our parents had since they didn't want us running away on them so early.

They knew we'd both want out of this town eventually and they were right; although, I had to promise them I'd come back after the summer.

They still don't believe that I will, but I've decided to at least give it a few more years before I make the big decision of leaving Arlington for good.

I'm hoping this visit to California doesn't make me break my promise, because that's the one thing I hate doing the most.

The next hour is spent tossing and turning before I finally make the decision to crawl out of bed to shower and finish packing.

My roommate won't be awake for at least another five hours, so we said our goodbyes last night over two cases of beer between us and three other friends, which *feels* like a huge mistake now. Literally.

On another note, it sucks that my parents are waiting outside to drive me to the airport in Madison, which is at least a thirty-minute drive.

Once I hear the Acadia pull into the driveway, I pick up my two bags—being extra careful with the one my laptop is tucked inside of—and begin making my way through the small house.

I'm surprised when Whitney mumbles something from behind me and throws her arms around my waist before I can make it to the front door.

"Whoa. I didn't expect to see you again for the next three months. What are you doing up?"

"You didn't really think I'd let you walk out that door without me being up to say goodbye, did you? I may feel like total shit, but I'm going to miss you like crazy and wanted to see you one last time before you leave. I also wanted to remind you to have fun, but not too much fun, got it?"

"Got it." I turn around and give her a tight hug. "I'm going to miss you too. Try not to have too much fun while I'm away. I'm sure Ethan will be living here the whole time I'm gone anyways, so you'll have plenty of fun to pass the time."

"Ha Ha. Aren't we funny," she mumbles. "Tell your brother hi for me, and I better have a damn good book to read about from your adventures once you return. You hear me?"

I nod and look over toward the door as it opens.

"Ready, Sweetheart?" My dad doesn't waste any time before walking over and grabbing my bags from me. "We're cutting it close already, and as much as we don't want you to leave, we don't want you missing your flight either."

I quickly tie my hair back and follow my dad to the door, stopping before I can walk outside. As boring as this place is, I really am going to miss Whitney over the next three months, and possibly even this crappy little house that I've finally gotten used to. "Alright. I'll message you tonight sometime. Don't miss me too much."

She laughs. "Just get out of here before I make my roomie stay or either squeeze my way into one of your bags and tag along for the summer."

"Yeah, I don't think Ethan would appreciate that or else I'd shove you inside myself. Later, babe." I smile and shut the door behind me, quickly jumping into the back of the red SUV.

Even though my dad looks as tired as I feel, my mother somehow looks upbeat and energetic, as if she's been awake for hours.

"We better be picking you back up from an airport in three months or you'll be breaking your father's heart. We already have one child living too far away. We don't need our baby girl running away on us too."

I lean back in the seat and get comfortable. "I know. I said I'd be back and I meant it, Mom." I yawn and close my eyes, wishing I was already on the plane, because I plan to sleep the entire way there. "Can you wake me up when we get there? I just need to keep my eyes closed."

"Is your brother picking you up from the airport?"

I shake my head.

"Why not?"

"*Vortex.*"

She huffs. "I hope he plans on taking a break while you're there. He works too hard."

"I'm sure he will, Mom. And besides, I'm a big girl now and I can take care of myself. I'll figure it out."

"I know, I know . . . I'll be quiet now so you can rest, seeing as you must have had a rough night last night."

I open one eye to see her shaking her head in disapproval, but she doesn't say anything else.

I take this as an opportunity to end the conversation and get some peace and quiet while I can . . .

Oceanside, California

EXCITEMENT COURSES THROUGH ME AS I toss my two bags into the first available taxi, before jumping inside and slamming the door shut behind me. The driver cusses under his breath, clearly not expecting me.

"Sorry," I say out of breath. "Take me here, please." I hold the small folded piece of paper over the front seat for the driver to grab.

He pulls it from my grip and opens it with a small, knowing smile. "Visiting Micah, I take it?"

I toss my bags beside me in the seat and crinkle my forehead in confusion. "Micah?" I question. "I have no idea who that is. I'm staying with my brother for the summer. This is the address he gave me, so I'm crossing my fingers that he wasn't dumb enough to give me the wrong one."

The man looks at me through the rearview mirror, before changing his tone and becoming a bit more professional. "My mistake, ma'am."

He pulls out into traffic, before speaking again. "So, you're

Alexander's sister?" he questions, while glancing at me in the mirror.

I smile. "His baby sister."

With Alexander owning a bar on the beach, the taxi driver knowing his name doesn't surprise me too much, but him knowing him by address . . . Yeah, a little weird.

"Is my brother a man-whore or something? Is that how you know his address? I know he doesn't go anywhere without his precious motorcycle, so I'm sure he has no need for a taxi himself," I say.

"Let's just say I've made a lot of early morning trips to his address."

"Gotcha," I say, grossed out. "No wonder he told me to enter with caution," I whisper under my breath.

A huge smile takes over my face when we finally pull up at my brother's beach house about twenty minutes later. I've wanted to visit him ever since he first moved here five years ago, but my parents wouldn't allow it, afraid that I wouldn't come back home. Xan had to come back to Wisconsin once every three months so we could see him and have family time.

Well damn . . . now I can see why.

"This is beautiful." I roll down the window and take a deep breath, taking in the salty air. "Oh my God. My brother is one lucky jerk."

The taxi driver smiles at me through the rearview mirror. "I don't disagree with you there, ma'am. What I wouldn't give to be in his shoes."

He stops the car and shifts it into park. "I hope you enjoy your summer here, ma'am."

"Tegan. Please don't call me ma'am. Makes me feel so old." I smile, grabbing my two bags. "No offense."

"It takes a lot to offend this old geezer." He shakes his head and pushes my hand away when I attempt to hand him money. "I can't take that. Your brother has been more than good to me. You just go and enjoy yourself."

"Thank you. That's nice of you . . ." I trail off, while searching for his name.

"The name's Tom," he says with a friendly smile.

"Perfect. Thanks, Tom." I toss him ten bucks as a tip and quickly take my bags, jumping out, before he can try and offer it back to me.

"Holy hell, my brother has been living the life while I've been stuck back home with my parents with nothing even remotely exciting to do."

Taking in the house, in total awe, I walk around to the back of the large house and I swear my breath gets knocked right out of me.

Hell, I even drop my bags, stunned.

There's a huge pool in the back, surrounded by a beautiful, lit up deck. Looking up at the house itself, I can see almost *everything*—huge sliding glass doors, large windows. There doesn't seem to be much privacy. Just a beautiful view, looking out at the oversized pool and beach.

"I hope my brother knows that I'm never leaving," I mumble, while picking my bags back up and making my way over to the door.

Just as I'm about to reach for the rock to get the key, a naked butt smashes against the glass in front of me and I scream, falling backwards.

"Oh my goodness! Holy shit!"

Placing my hand over my chest, I look up with squinted eyes to see that the tan butt is really there. It wasn't just my imagination playing a cruel joke on me like I'd hoped.

My eyes slowly ascend the site before me, watching, as a guy holds the butt in place while he shamelessly pounds into some girl right in front of my face.

I quickly scramble to my feet, my eyes meeting *his* baby blue ones as strands of long, dark hair falls into his face.

I expect him to stop screwing *her*, but instead, he just pounds into her even harder, while making sure to keep eye contact with me.

After a few seconds, he pulls his gaze away from mine and bites the girl's neck, causing her to slam her head back into the glass.

This gives me the strength I need to cover my face and turn the other way. "I'm going to kill my brother!"

Growling in frustration, I reach for my phone and start walking toward the beach to get away from the action.

This was not the action I was seeking by coming here for the summer. I didn't ask for a woman's naked butt in my face.

I call my brother and he answers it on the third ring.

"What the hell, Xan?"

"Shit," he mumbles. "I'm taking it Micah's there?"

"Oh! So, this Micah guy does exist. Good to know, dumbass. Especially since I just walked up on his dirty little screw-fest against the back door. Some woman's butt was in my face. Her *naked* butt. That's so not cool, Xan."

He laughs a little. He actually fucking laughs.

"Sorry. I didn't think he'd be back already, so I wasn't sure. That's why I told you to enter with caution. He wasn't supposed to be back home for another few days, but you never know with him."

Walking through the sand, I finally stop and take a seat, kicking my shoes off. "Why didn't you mention this Micah guy before? I didn't even know you had a roommate."

"Hang on . . ." The noise around him starts to die down. I assume he's walking to his office so he can hear me better. "He has his own place, but I like him there to keep an eye on things since I'm not around much. He's the closest I have to family here and one of the only people I fully trust. He goes back and forth from my place to his. He's sort of made the downstairs area his."

"Then please tell me I'll be sleeping upstairs. I'm afraid to touch anything down there after what I just witnessed. I might even need to sanitize my eyeballs."

"Yes," he says firmly, all playfulness gone from his voice. "I want you close to me and *away* from Micah. He's my friend and I trust him, but not with you. Far from that shit."

I let out a relieved breath and stand back up, brushing the sand off. "Good, I'm sure there'll be no problem there. Now, when will you be home? It feels like it's been forever since I've seen you."

"Give me two hours or so and I'll be there. I'll call Micah and tell him to open the front door for you."

"Yeah . . . good, since I won't be going anywhere near that back door *ever* again. That might be best."

"Gotta go. Get settled in and I'll see you later."

"Later, Xan."

Hanging up the phone, I close my eyes and the first thing that takes over my thoughts is the way *Micah's* intense eyes watched *me* while he was having sex with another girl.

It sent chills down my spine, and almost turned me on, although, I'll never admit that to anyone.

I'm so embarrassed by it. I've never watched anyone having sex before and I wasn't planning on it anytime soon, that's for sure.

Giving Micah some time to finish his business, I stay on the beach for another twenty minutes or so enjoying the peacefulness, before walking back to the house and *praying* with everything in me, that there isn't a naked butt plastered to the door this time.

"Why the hell did I leave my bags around back?" I scold myself, realizing I'll have to go back to that stupid door to retrieve my things.

Once I get to the house I look around for my bags, but don't see them anywhere. I make my way around to the front of the house to see that the door is unlocked for me.

"Thank God." I push the door open and step into the house, surprised when I look over at the couch to see Micah naked with a guitar sitting in his lap.

He stops playing and looks over at me, not even bothering to act surprised that I just walked in on him naked. If I didn't know any better I'd say he stayed in the nude just to get another reaction out of me.

"I put your bags upstairs in your room," he says, before going back to relaxing and playing his guitar as if I'm not even here.

"I'm guessing you don't own any clothes?" I question sarcastically.

As hard as I try, I can't stop my eyes from taking in every inch of his exposed body. It screams trouble with every rock-hard muscle.

"Oh, I do." He looks up at me with a steeled jaw. "I just prefer not to wear them." He lifts a brow, looking my body over. "Want me to show you to your room?"

I let out an annoyed laugh. "No, thanks. Looks like you have a hard enough time finding your own."

My heart speeds up with unwanted excitement as his eyes continue to rake down my body. He slides his lip between his teeth, letting out a small growl.

God, that's a sexy lip . . .

Shaking my head, I clear my throat and pull myself together, before he can get any wrong ideas of what might be happening while I'm here for the summer. "Thanks for grabbing my bags. I'll be upstairs *alone* settling in."

Before he can say anything, I jog up the stairs and find the room with my bags in it.

It's huge. Much bigger than any room I've had back home, and even though I know I'm going to love it here, I can't help but to ask myself . . .

Why the hell does my brother have to have such a hot roommate?

Now he's really on my shit list.

Chapter Two

Micah

AFTER ALEXANDER'S LITTLE SISTER WENT to her room last night, *alone,* I went to *Vortex* for a few drinks, just to fucking get chewed out by my best friend for doing what I do best.

How the hell was I supposed to know she'd be coming in through the back door? And how was I supposed to know she'd be so damn hot, making me wish it were her against the door?

Alexander made it clear last night that I'm to stay away from his baby sister.

Good job, dude. You just found a way to make me crave having sex with her even more.

I'm in my office, getting things ready for the day, when Gavin knocks on the door, looking scared to take on his first day.

"Where do I start, Sir?"

Shutting down my computer, I spin around in my chair and look him over. "You can start by losing the damn shirt. You won't need one while working here."

"Right." He nods, pulling his shirt over his head. "I forgot."

"Follow me and I'll take you to Colby. He'll train you for a few hours and then you're on your own. Think you can handle that?"

"Yes, Sir."

"Don't call me sir, Gavin." I walk past him, motioning for him to follow me. "It makes me feel fucking old. It's Micah and nothing else."

"Sorry," he says apologetically. "Thanks for giving me this opportunity. I've had friends on the waiting list for over a year now. I was expecting to have to wait longer than five months to get in."

"You can thank your baby face for the job. Women go crazy for guys like you around here. We needed to replace our last baby-faced bartender. Now we just need to see if you can perform your job. That will determine whether or not we'll need a replacement for a third time, so don't mess up."

"Got it . . . uh . . . Micah," he stammers. "I won't let you down."

"Good to fucking hear."

Once downstairs, I spot Colby sitting on his knees on the bar, while some chick shoves money into the front of his jeans. "Are you a stripper or a bartender?" I question, causing him to cuss under his breath at being caught. "I can send your ass to *Walk of Shame* if you'd like, but you'd have to be willing to move to Chicago. I'm sure my cousin Slade could get you in."

"My bad. She asked for it." He smirks, while jumping behind the bar and looking Gavin over. "Our baby face replacement?"

I nod. "Have him ready to be on his own by five and don't teach him any of your half-assed shit. Train him by the book."

He looks him over once again. "I'll do my best, Boss."

I'm about to walk back up to my office when I spot Sebastian sitting at one of the tables drinking.

"That little shit . . ."

Angry, I throw my arm around Ryan and point at the kid. "Did you serve him again, Ry?"

Ryan swallows hard, while looking over to see who I'm pointing at. "Yeah. He had an ID. I checked—"

"Go home," I say firmly.

"But . . . how was I supposed to know it was a fake?"

Pissed off, I get in his face, causing him to back up a step. "Because it's the third fucking time you've been told not to serve him. Now get your shit and go home."

Walking away from Ryan before I lose my shit over his stupidity, I make my way toward Sebastian and drag him to his feet. "What the hell did I tell you about coming here, Sebastian?"

"Micah," he groans. "Come on, Man. I'm almost eighteen. Stop treating me like a child."

"You *are* a child," I spit out. "You should be worried about surfing and girls, *not* how many damn beers you can finish before I spot your ass in the crowd."

He attempts to reach for his beer as I drag him away from the table and out the door, but just ends up knocking it off the table instead.

Once outside, I drag him over to the sand and toss him down.

"Dammit, Sebastian." I grip my hair in frustration, while looking down at him. "I've been trying my best to keep my patience with you, but you keep testing my ass. Get your shit together, because I won't always be here to bail your ass out of everything. Got it?"

"Yeah . . ." He jumps to his feet and wipes the back of his shorts off. "I never asked you to bail me out of anything, and I definitely never asked you to act like you're my damn dad."

My eyes meet his as I step closer to him. "You want me to stop? Because I guarantee with the life you've been living that your ass would be *dead* in less than two weeks." I fix his shirt for him. "Now get your shit together, Sebastian. Get out of here."

"Whatever, Dude," he mumbles. "I'll see you later."

Worried about the kid, I watch as he runs through the sand and over to his little group of friends who high-five him and toss him something to drink. Most likely a beer.

"Fuuuuck. This kid never stops."

I really need to get him away from those little low-lives. They're no good for him, but they're all that he's had his whole life, since his parents have never given a shit about what he does.

I've been dealing with him sneaking into *Vortex* for two years now and I've been doing my best to help him get his head on straight.

The kid thinks I'll give up on him just like his parents did. He's wrong.

"Oh look. You do own clothing after all," a sarcastic voice says from behind me.

I'd know that sweet voice from anywhere, and I have to admit that I spent most of the night imagining what she'd sound like screaming from below me. Or on top . . . whatever she's in the mood for.

"I wasn't lying, babe." Smirking, I turn around to find Tegan sitting at one of the outdoor tables with her laptop. "This is just the only place I wear them. They're sort of required here." I tilt my head and watch as her eyes wander over my body. She's trying to play it off, as if it's not obvious she's picturing me naked, but the quiver of her bottom lip gives her away. "So, I don't own many."

"I'm sure that seems to work for you," she mumbles.

"It does; although, I usually get asked to take my clothes off here as well." I walk over to the table and peer over her shoulder, curious. "Still Breathing . . ." I smile as she stiffens. "Are you writing a book?"

Clearing her throat, she turns around and palms my face, pushing it back. "Do you mind? I can't think with you so close."

"That doesn't sound like a bad thing," I tease.

Grunting, she closes her laptop. "Yes."

"Yes?" I question. "That it's a bad thing?"

"That I'm writing a book." Her eyes wander over my body again, stopping on my chest. "Why are you wearing a shirt?"

"Would you prefer I take it off for you?"

She laughs sarcastically. "I think I saw enough of your body last night to keep my mind busy for a while, thank you." She smiles up at Gavin and thanks him as he drops a drink off at her table. "I asked because every guy here is shirtless, with the exception of you. Is that a thing here? My brother left that juicy little detail out. Shirtless, sexy bartender heaven. I have a feeling I'm going to like it here."

"All the bartenders are required to be shirtless, yes, but I'm not bartending or playing right now."

"Playing?" she questions. "Your guitar?"

"You can come watch me tonight if you want to know. I'm pretty sure that isn't against the rules."

Opening her laptop again, she looks up at me and laughs. "Rules?"

Letting out a small breath, I give her a serious look and pull my shit together, before I somehow manage to break these damn *rules*. "Your brother's," I say firmly. "Should you need me if my boys don't attend to you and take care of you like you deserve, I'll be upstairs in my office. Don't be afraid to tell me if they slack."

"My brother is funny," she says softly, watching me as I back away from her and turn around to leave.

Her words stop me. "How so?"

"For thinking he can control me while I'm here. Last time I checked I was a grown woman who makes her own decisions."

"Yeah," I mumble. "Well, good luck telling your brother that."

With that, I walk away, leaving her outside, *alone,* to work on her book. Something about leaving her alone here with shirtless men is bothering me. Maybe it's the fact that I know she likes it. Or the fact that I know they'll want her, and unlike me, they might have a chance of touching her.

Out of nowhere, a pair of hands press against my chest and begin feeling me up. "You're wearing too much clothing, Micah," Gwen says against my ear, as she trails her hand down to grab my junk.

Growling, I grip her hand, making her grab it tighter.

"Mmmm . . ." she moans. "Is somebody ready to play?"

"No," I whisper, just below her ear. "I'm reminding you of what you'll never feel in your mouth again." I push her hand away. "Now keep your hands to yourself or I'll have you escorted out."

"Micah," she huffs. "Don't act like you don't miss me. No one else will *ever* do the things that *I* do."

"Then they'll probably last longer," I say stiffly. "Now, I've got shit to do."

"Fuck off, Micah." She straightens out her skirt, seeming embarrassed. "You'll be back."

"Nope. I won't," I say, keeping my cool. "I'm needed in my office. Go cling to Colby. He actually enjoys it."

Without giving her a chance to respond I walk away, jogging up the steps to my office.

One time, over a year ago, and Gwen keeps coming back for more, thinking that I'll give her what she wants. She wants a man she can control.

That's not me.

Just as I'm opening my office door, Alexander walks out of his, closing the door behind him.

"Dude, have you been here all morning?" I question, looking his tired ass over.

He runs a hand through his messy, dark hair and yawns. "Yeah, got here bright and early to take care of some shit."

Opening my office, I enter, knowing that Xan will follow.

"Well, you look like hell."

Alexander smiles. "Thanks for the obvious, Asshole." He closes the door behind him and takes a seat in the chair across from me. "I saw my sister walk in. Will you keep your eye on her, Man? I need to get some sleep before tonight."

"You're trusting me to keep an eye on her?" I laugh and place my hands behind my head, lifting a brow to him.

"Fuck no," he grumbles. "But what other choice do I have? There's a lot of assholes around here that will try to pick her up. At least make me feel somewhat better that you'll be here."

"Yeah, Man," I say, while watching the cameras. "I'll keep the assholes away."

Alexander stands up. "Yourself included," he says sternly. "My sister is a good girl. She deserves a good man that will take care of her, not someone to just show her one night of pleasure and kick her to the curb. Promise me, Micah."

Hearing the worry in his voice causes me to look up and truly see how much this means to him. The last thing I want to do is piss my best friend off and lose his trust. He's had my back for years now. More than anyone else has.

"Yeah, Man. Myself included." I point at my door. "Now get the hell out of my office, Dick."

"On it. I'll be back in a few hours."

After Alexander leaves, I sit back and watch Tegan, ready to protect her from any asshole that tries to pick her up on my watch.

Myself included.

Shit, this is going to be harder than I expected . . .

Chapter Three

Tegan

HE COMES AT ME SLOWLY, sweat dripping from his hard body.

"No," I grunt, while hitting backspace.

He comes at me slowly, sweat dripping from every rock-hard muscle. His eyes trail over my bare flesh as if he's ready to taste every exposed inch of me.

"Whoa! Whoa! What the hell are you writing?"

My brother's voice scares me, causing my heart to nearly jump to my throat. I didn't have a chance to see him last night since he's been so busy, and he decides to choose the worst possible time to show up out of nowhere.

Figures.

"What the hell, Xan!" I slam my computer shut and spin around to face him. "Didn't anyone ever teach you not to read over someone's shoulder? You don't do that shit. I was in deep concentration. Now you just messed up the flow of the scene."

"My bad," he mumbles, while opening his soda. "Didn't mean to disturb the porn scene in your head, little sis."

"Oh, come on. That's gross. Don't ever let me hear that word come from your lips again."

He eyes me over his can, while taking a long drink of his soda. I almost think he's never going to stop for air. All that acid at once has to burn.

"What are you doing here, anyway? I thought you were writing at the bar."

"I was," I complain. "Until Micah sent me home."

Xan smirks, before finishing the rest of his soda off. "Oh yeah? Why?"

My brother looks entirely *too* happy right now. I'm guessing he had something to do with Micah popping by my table every damn time a guy showed up.

"Because the bartenders kept trying to pick me up. I wasn't getting anything done, apparently. At least that's what Micah said when he picked up my computer and sent me packing."

"Good boy," he whispers.

"What?"

"Nothing." He kisses me on the head and walks back over to the door, stopping to look back at me. "I need to get back to the bar. Micah plays in an hour and I need to take over the staff. Those boys are fucking trouble unless you watch them twenty-four-seven. No lie. I promise we'll do lunch or dinner soon and catch up."

The image of Micah playing his guitar, naked, takes over my thoughts, and suddenly, writing can wait. I need to be at the bar to see him play.

I came here for entertainment and I have a feeling that he's going to take the spotlight.

"I'll be there then," I say, opening my laptop back up. "I'll just finish this scene and head out."

"I thought you wanted to get your book done," he quips with amusement. "Instead, you'd rather stress my ass out by hanging around at my bar full of horny jerkoffs?"

I take a second to think his words over. "Yeah. Isn't that what siblings are for? Maybe you should've thought about that *before* you decided to open a bar full of hot, shirtless men serving beer. Just saying."

He grunts. "I was hoping to keep you away for as long as I could. Just bring Jamie with you so you're not alone. She's been dying for you to get here. Call her."

"Good idea. I haven't seen her since she moved."

"I guess I'll see you soon. Just don't fall for their stupid games. I'm serious. My guys are trouble." He waves his hand at me, before rushing out of my room and down the stairs.

After he leaves, I stare at my computer for a good twenty minutes, but the words won't come. "Damn you, Xan."

I shut my computer down and call Jamie, before changing into a pair of comfortable shorts and a tank top, with a bikini underneath.

The best thing about my brother's bar is that you can drink a few beers and get a little tipsy, before running down to the beach to get wet and play in the water.

You can't beat that . . .

ONCE JAMIE ARRIVES WE DO a little catching up on the last three years, before walking down to the beach and heading toward *Vortex*.

"I can't believe you're finally here. Do you have any idea how bored I've been without you?" Jamie asks, holding her blonde hair out of her face as the wind blows it everywhere, causing her to eat it while she talks.

Waving my arms around me, I laugh at her for even thinking she can trick me into believing that crap. "I'm sure you've been *so* bored without me; spending time on this beautiful beach, full of sexy, half-naked men. I have no idea how you've managed this long without me," I tease.

She grins as a hot guy jogs past us, chasing after a Frisbee. "You're right. I totally lied. Check out the abs on that one." She lifts a brow, inspecting him. "But seriously though, you're here now and we're going to have a blast. I'll make sure of it."

Her words have me smiling, but my mind drifts to Micah, and suddenly, I'm curious.

"Do you know this Micah guy that my brother hangs out with?"

She stops dead in her tracks and starts fanning herself. "Who the hell doesn't? He's the sexiest man to hold a guitar." When I turn back around, she's following me again. "He's pretty well known around here. For both his looks and his talent."

"Yeah? But what do you know about him personally?"

She shrugs her shoulders. "I don't know. Not much. Just that he's been friends with Xan for a while now and that he moved here alone from Chicago. From what I hear, he's saving up to open his own bar. One where live music is a nightly thing."

"Yeah, well my brother failed to mention him to me, and I can't help but wonder why. Especially the fact that he practically lives with him. What the hell is that about? We used to be close."

Jamie shakes her head. "I'm not sure, but I have a pretty good idea."

"Oh yeah? Why?"

"Look at you. You're gorgeous, talented and young. Then look at Micah. Also gorgeous, talented and young. And he gets any and every girl his little heart desires. I'm sure he just wanted to keep you at a distance, worried that you'd fall for him and get hurt." She claps excitedly once the bar comes into view. "Look at this crowd tonight. It's the busiest on the nights that he plays."

"Wow!" I look around in surprise at how much the bar filled up in such a short amount of time. It's a huge change from this afternoon. "This is pretty amazing. I'm excited now. He must put on a good show to attract this many people."

"Oh honey . . . his voice is orgasmic. Let's hurry and grab a few drinks so we can get a spot close to the stage. If there are any left."

While walking up to the outside bar, my brother spots me from the other side and nods to me, before continuing his conversation with a group of girls that are practically hanging all over him.

"Go over to Colby's side. He's faster," Jamie says, pulling me through the crowd. "And he's the hottest one here besides Micah and your brother."

"My brother?" I roll my eyes and stick close to her until we make our way up to Colby.

"Yeah, your brother. He's extremely *hot*." She shivers. "Those tattoos and abs make me want to run my tongue all over every inch of his hard body."

"Gross, Jamie! I did not need to hear that."

As soon as Colby notices me, he leans over the bar and grabs my hand, pulling my attention away from Jamie. "You ready for that date, babe?"

Smiling, I pull my hand out of his. "Nice try, playboy. How about a beer instead?"

"Make that two," Jamie chimes in. "And can you get them from the *furthest* back?"

Lifting a brow, he walks over to the cooler and bends down.

"Mmmm . . ." Jamie moans. "Keep looking, stud. We want

the coldest ones. Dig deeper. Much deeper."

A minute later, Colby turns around, holding two beers in his hand. "Did you girls enjoy the view?" he asks, smirking, while sliding our beers in front of us.

"Very much so. Your ass is fantastic," Jamie responds. She grabs her beer and tosses some cash down. "Thanks. Keep the change."

I don't even get a chance to throw down a tip myself, before she grabs my arm and starts pulling me back through the crowd.

The last couple of tables close to the stage are now crowded with people, but when we get past that crowd, I see Micah leaning against a table that sits right in front of the stage.

As our eyes meet, he nods, and mouths for me to come to him.

Watching those lips move and having to focus on them to see what he's saying only makes me notice more just how damn sexy they truly are.

"Over here." I tug Jamie toward the table Micah's leaning against.

With his arms crossed over his chest, he watches me the whole time. I do mean every single step.

"Your brother told me you were coming." He uncrosses his arms and pulls out the chairs for us. "I'll be keeping my eye on you."

Keeping his gaze glued to mine, he slowly yanks his shirt over his head, as if doing a strip tease, and tosses it down, before walking away and heading to the stage.

"Damn," Jamie says with wide eyes. "Can he keep his eyes on me like that, please? What was that about? And did he just strip for you?"

"No. That was not for me." I shrug my shoulders and take a seat, my heart still racing from the look in his eyes as he stripped his shirt off. "Him and my stupid brother are being overly protective, as if I can't handle a few horny bartenders. That's all."

She takes a sip of her beer while watching Micah take a seat and tune his guitar. The way his long hair flows over his shoulders has it impossible to take your eyes away. "I'm staying at your place tonight," she says, not bothering to look at me when she speaks. "I promise not to stare too hard at the boys."

Rolling my eyes, I tilt back my beer and set my eyes on the stage, then kick my sandals off. "You're not good at keeping promises," I mumble.

"Doesn't keep me from making them," she teases.

"Good to see you, Jamie."

Jamie looks up from the sound of my brother's voice close by, blushing.

He's standing right behind her, peering over her shoulder; so close that their bodies are touching.

She swallows, before pulling herself together. "Good to see you too, Alexander. It's been a few months."

"You're looking good. Glad to see you're back home." He walks over to me and hands me some kind of pager type thing. "Push this if you need anything. It's connected to Colby's buzzer. I don't want you fighting your way through the crowd every time you girls need a drink."

"Seriously?" I look down at the buzzer. "That's all we have to do?"

"VIP . . . little sis. I got you ladies." He rubs the top of my head. "Just don't fucking abuse it or I'll have to take it away. Got me?" Smiling, he backs away. "Enjoy the show."

I can't help but to laugh when the girls clearly check him out as he rushes past them to get some work done, or whatever it is that he's in a hurry to do.

"Dude . . . your brother is pretty awesome. You know that, right?"

"I guess," I mumble, smiling. "It's a good thing I take after him then, right?"

Jamie shrugs. "Eh."

"Screw off!" Laughing, I toss my beer label at her and then freeze when Micah speaks into the mic, getting the attention of the crowd.

"Are you ladies ready?"

The crowd screams. Myself included.

"Damn," he smirks, before looking around, his eyes landing on me. "It's not often I make the ladies scream while still wearing my jeans. I can't imagine how loud it'd be if I weren't wearing these."

The girls start screaming even louder, yelling at him to take his jeans off.

I stay quiet this time, even though inside I wish they were off too.

"Sorry, ladies. We have rules here . . . unfortunately." He laughs into the mic and it's so damn deep and sexy that I shift in my seat and sip my beer to distract myself. "I'm feeling like some Shinedown tonight. Here's one of my favorites. It's called *I Dare You.*"

The crowd quiets down as soon as he starts playing and all eyes are on him.

I honestly can't pull my eyes away as I watch his fingers move, pulling the strings of his guitar.

The way the muscles in his arms flex as he plays has me completely zoning in on him. Every part of him.

Until his lips move and the most beautiful sound comes out, working me up and instantly causing me to sweat.

It's crazy just how good he really is.

"He's soooooo good," Jamie points out. "I feel like it's been forever since I heard him play. We need to come here every week together while you're here. You game?"

Needing another drink to hopefully calm my now racing thoughts, I press the buzzer.

A few times.

"You need another beer? I need another beer. Is it hot out here?" I say quickly. "I need out of this stupid shirt."

In a hurry to cool off, I pull my shirt off and set it down next to me in my seat.

"Better?" Jamie questions with amusement.

"Yeah." Micah is now watching me as he sings. There are probably a hundred girls in this damn crowd, yet he's looking right the hell at me, as if he can't look away. "No." I shake my head. "Not really. I think I'm having a heatstroke or something. I need liquid and fast."

Colby appears over my shoulder, nearly scaring the crap out of me as he holds out two beers. "You know . . . this is almost like calling me, which you can do later tonight."

"Oh, is it? I bet you say that to all the girls that hold this special buzzer," Jamie teases. "It's a shame we didn't get to watch you fetch these beers though."

"You're telling me, babe. I feel sorry for you both." He winks at me and then backs away when Micah glares at him from the stage.

It's easy to see who the boss is around here, because Colby instantly walks away and returns to work.

Micah's gaze lands on me for a few short seconds, before finally turning away to look down at his guitar.

Knowing that Whitney will kill me if she knows I watched a hot guy perform at my brother's bar and not capture it, I take a quick photo to send to her.

A text comes through from her a few minutes later.

Whitney: Holy-beautiful-long-haired babe. He is gorgeous. I wonder if Ethan would be pissed if I make this my screensaver. I guess we'll see . . .

I laugh at her response but tuck my phone away, not wanting to miss any of Micah's performance.

He plays three more songs, causing the crowd to fall more and more in love with him and his voice. He then says goodnight to everyone and hops off the stage to grab a water bottle and pour it over his sweat-covered body.

His eyes lock with mine as he rubs the water down his chest and arms, before reaching for his shirt and walking away through the crowd.

I swear he gets stopped every step that he takes. These women are ready to eat him alive. Literally. I think one even tried to lick him when he walked past her.

It's ridiculous.

"What the hell?" I finish off my last beer and stand up. "Are the women always like this around here?"

Jamie stands up and stretches. "Not always." She smiles. "They're worse sometimes. I swear you'd think this was a strip club the way they feel all over these boys."

"Interesting," I whisper. "I should just write about my brother's damn bar."

"You should," she responds. "Do you have any idea how much action goes on around here?"

"Nope. My brother doesn't tell me shit."

She grins like a madman. "Well, you're about to see some shit this summer. Let's get out of here." She tosses her empty bottle in the nearby trash. "I have to work for a few hours tomorrow morning."

"Yeah," I agree. "I need to get some writing done."

WHEN I GET BACK TO my brother's house, I grab my laptop and bring it out back by the pool.

I've been writing for a good hour, suddenly feeling inspired, before a splash causes me to jerk back and look up.

Standing up, I glance into the pool to see a hard, muscled back, swimming through the water.

My gaze stays glued to Micah's back, until he emerges from the water, exposing his toned, naked butt.

"Holy shit! Come on, Micah," I scream, as he climbs out of the pool while covering his junk with both of his hands. "Why are you naked . . . again?"

"A little warning," he whispers next to my ear. "Stay away from the pool after I get home from playing." He moves in closer, his lips brushing under my ear. "Unless you want to get *wet*."

My entire body quivers as I watch him walk away and let himself into the house.

Why does his body and hair being wet have to make him even sexier?

I'm angry that he treats me this way, yet so damn turned on by it.

Maybe I'm just angry at myself.

Angry at myself for wanting his body so damn bad, knowing that I can't have it . . .

Strung is Available Now

Continue on to read the prologue and first chapter of CLAIMED by Jenika Snow.

Excerpt from *Claimed* by Jenika Snow

PROLOGUE

Claire

I SHIVERED, THE THIN GOWN I was wearing barely keeping the chill off my body. I couldn't see much aside from the bright lights that illuminated the stage. There were several other women behind me, some of them crying, others so emotionless I wondered if they were already broken.

All of us were property.

This was the world I lived in, where being a fertile female made me someone else's property.

I knew out there, in the crowd hidden behind shadows, were wealthy men of all ages. They'd purchase us, do whatever they wanted with us. We'd be nothing but chattel to them, a shiny new toy for them to use . . . to abuse. The society I lived in was barbaric, where humans could be taken against their will and sold off to someone who had the right amount of coin.

That thought had fear freezing my body.

How I wished I lived in a time where this was only read about in fiction, where it wasn't a reality. How I wished I could go to the past, where society wasn't fucked-up and people weren't starving.

Would the person who purchased me use me as a sex slave, strictly to get them off? Or maybe they'd use me as a breeder, a vessel to carry their heir and pass on their lineage. Either way, all I wanted to do was run off the stage and escape, but I knew I wouldn't make it. I knew I would be captured before I even got to the front doors.

I felt my hands shaking, and soon my entire body followed suit. It was a silent auction, one where I wouldn't know who purchased me until it was far too late.

It was already too late.

And so I closed my eyes, focusing on something else, somewhere else. I thought about the small camp of "runaways" I'd been staying with, men and women who were against how the world was, how the government could sell humans as if they were nothing more than a new toy.

I stood there, my eyes closed, my thoughts on being free, on being alone in the woods where I could pretend that where I was, wasn't the end of the line for me. I didn't know how long I stood there, not focused on anything but myself, but I finally felt someone take hold of my arm and cart me offstage.

I was led into the back hallways, pushed into a room where I was changed into a thicker gown, my feet shoved into flats, my hair haphazardly put into a messy bun. I had a bracelet snapped around my wrist, a number etched all around it . . . my new owner's purchase number.

And so it is. I am a piece of property.

Once I was dressed and ready for my hell-on-earth future, I was again led toward the back. There I saw two double doors wide open, the breeze washing over me and almost making me cry. I could see the woods just behind, so close yet so far away. I wanted to run, but I didn't want to make this harder on myself. I didn't want to make my life even more miserable than I knew it already would be.

It can't get any worse. Death would be far more humane.

And then, once I was outside, I tugged on the two men leading me. They tightened their holds until the pain lanced up my arms. There, waiting no more than a few feet from me, was a dark car, shiny, reeking of money. The back door was opened by what I could only assume was a servant of the man awaiting me inside. God, would he be old? Would he be gentle or cruel and violent to me?

Nothing was said, no words spoken. I was, after all, nothing more than chattel to them.

Once in the car, my eyes adjusted to the darkness. I could see his big body across from me, the shadows partially hiding his face. My heart was beating so fast, and I felt sweat start to cover my body in fearful beads of emotion.

The vehicle started moving, and I curled my hands into tight fists, afraid to breathe, let alone say anything. And then he leaned forward, the light finally making a swatch across his face. He was brutally handsome, with dark hair and even darker eyes. I saw the tattoos that covered his body, not something that was practiced much anymore, but seeming to make my heart beat harder, painfully fast.

He was older, maybe in his thirties, still much older than my mere twenty years. But he appeared wiser, as if he'd seen more than he should have, experienced more than he'd wanted to.

And then he leaned forward, grabbed my hand in his much bigger one, and I swear I felt fire kick across my skin. The cuff of his jacket rode up slightly, and I saw the tattoos painting his wrist and creeping up his forearm.

I was frozen in place, my muscles tensed, not knowing what he was going to do. He stared into my eyes, his so dark, so deep. Who was this man? Why was he making me feel like I was on edge? Why was he making me feel aroused with just a touch? I should be disgusted by him, frightened because I had no idea what he would do to me.

But he said nothing, his big body making me feel so small, so vulnerable. And then, before I could realize what he was doing, he tore the property bracelet from my wrist. I felt my eyes widen as I realized what he'd just done. That simple act was one of re-bellion. I was not his property, and he'd made that clear without saying one word.

Without saying anything, he leaned back, swallowed by the shadows of the interior of the car once more.

My heart thundered so hard and fast, worse than when I'd stood on that auction block not knowing what my future held. The car ride seemed endless. But eventually we were slowing and I glanced out the tinted window to see a massive estate coming into view. Although I wasn't looking at the man, I could feel his gaze on me, like tendrils of fire moving along my skin. It was as if he was reaching out and stroking my arms with his fingertips. But I refused to look at him. He might have taken off the bracelet, but that didn't mean I knew what was going to happen or if he would let me go. I could've laughed at my thoughts.

Let me go? No doubt he paid an exorbitant amount of money for me.

The vehicle came to a stop, and I sat there, my breathing increasing as I thought about all the horrible things that might happen once I stepped inside that house.

"You're safe," the man finally said, his voice so deep, so mas-culine I felt it race up my spine.

I looked at him then. He leaned forward so the light moved along his face once more.

"No one will ever hurt you again. I'll make sure you're pro-tected and healed properly; then after that, you're free to go."

I felt my eyes widen. "Free to go?" I whispered. Although I wanted to escape, I also knew I didn't have anywhere safe to run to. The chances of being caught again played through my head like a horror movie.

"Yes. I can set you up in a safe house once I know you'll be protected and they can't find you again."

I couldn't believe what was happening right now. "I don't understand." I could have cried, and in fact I felt a single tear slip out of the corner of my eye.

"We can talk about this more once you're inside, a change of clothes covering you, and a warm meal in your belly."

I felt dizzy, like if I stood right now, I might faint. He helped me out of the vehicle and all I could do was lean on him for support, not sure if I was dreaming or if this was reality. I looked up at him, his body so much bigger than mine. Could this be real? Could I actually be . . . free?

★ ★ ★

SHE'S MINE.

Those words slammed into my head over and over again, a derailed train about to crash and destroy anything and everything in its path. I couldn't control it, couldn't stop the deep rumble that came from me. I could see her eyes widen farther, the blues so startling they made my heart slam harder in my chest. The long fall of her blonde hair had my hands twitching, my fingers tingling. I wanted to touch the locks, wanted to see if they felt as soft as they looked.

What's wrong with me?

I exhaled slowly, reining in my control. I wasn't about to lose my shit. I couldn't, not in front of her.

My words had shocked her. It was unbelievable to her, I was sure. I had purchased her just to set her free. But as I stared at her, something in me shifted. I didn't want to set her free, not because

I was a sadistic bastard, but because for the first time in my life I finally felt something come alive in me.

It had taken one look, one sound of her voice, and this possessive side in me came forth like a dangerous beast. I was doing everything in my power to be calm, to keep collected and be stoic. No need to frighten her further. She needed to earn my trust, know that I wouldn't hurt her.

But despite all of that, I could only think about was how I wanted.

She is mine. She will be mine.

And as those words beat in my head like a war drum, a song before a battle, I knew she was different. She was so very different from any woman I'd ever seen, ever known.

Mine.

"What's your name?" My voice was thick, scratchy. I'd kept in the shadows of the car, watching her, seeing her reaction play across her face. She licked her lips, and I lowered my gaze to watch the act.

"Claire," she said in the sweetest, softest voice I'd ever heard, a song from the very heavens above.

My body became tense, my blood rushing through my veins. I wanted to protect her, to kill anyone who ever hurt her, who dared to even think about doing so. I wanted blood on my hands, bodies at my feet. It would all be in the name of Claire. I'd always been protective of the women I saved, but this was different. Where I felt an almost parental connection to those woman, a part of me wanting to care for them because they'd had such a rough go at life, with Claire I felt something much more personal. I was protective of her, territorial of her, not only because I wanted to make sure she was safe, but because I wanted her as my own.

I watched her, not saying anything for long seconds. When I finally felt in control and knew I could say anything without sounding like a ravished animal, I spoke. "I'm Xavier . . ."

And you're mine.

ONE

Xavier

One month later

IN THE LAST MONTH I'D been watching her like a fiend. Never had I desired a woman as much as I did her.

There hadn't been a woman in years.

Claire was sweet and gentle, innocent and vulnerable.

The world we lived in was cruel, stripping away at females until there was nothing left but skin and bones. I was thirty-five years old, and for the last decade I'd used my wealth and power to help countless women find a life outside of servitude.

After seeing my mother used and abused, I'd made it my mission to help women so they didn't turn out just like she had. And when my father died ten years ago and I inherited his estate and fortune, I'd begun helping every woman I could. Didn't matter that I'd purchased dozens of women over the years. In fact, our society didn't care if I owned a fucking harem as long as I could pay.

And I could pay until I died of old age. Hell, my descendants could keep paying until they died of old age, and so on and so forth.

I had work to do, a lot of fucking work, but I couldn't help but think about Claire. I stood and walked over to the window. Although the weather was chilly, a frost settling over everything, she still went out every day. I had a feeling she did so despite the weather because of her fear of imprisonment, because for so long she hadn't been able to be free in any way that counted.

But it didn't matter how many times I told her she was not a prisoner, that the only reason she was here was because I had to make sure it was safe for her to be on her own. I could still see that fear and uncertainty in her eyes.

And I hated seeing that look on her face, even when I told her that I had to get affairs in order first, but then, after that, she should be safe, free to live her life the way she wanted to.

But a part of me, a very strong one, didn't want her to go. I would not keep her as a prisoner, wouldn't do it against her will, but I wanted her here with me. I wanted her by my side, in my bed. I wanted her as mine.

I leaned against the wall and stared out the window at the gardens. I couldn't help but watch her all the time, fascinated by every aspect of her. Claire was unlike any woman I'd ever met. She was intelligent, and I knew she was fearless, even though she kept to herself. I could see her taking everything in, storing it, memorizing.

She was intuitive, her natural instinct telling her to be wary. It was that survival instinct that had allowed her to last as long as she had on her own.

And then she looked over at me and my heart froze, my body stilling. Everything inside of me told me to go claim her right then and there, to pull her close to my body so no one could touch her, hurt her. I wanted to wrap her up and make sure she was safe, that she never saw the horrors of this fucked-up world again.

Her eyes were so big, her look so vulnerable. She seemed so unsure of what was happening. God, the things she'd probably seen and experienced, the life she'd led. I wished I could turn back time so she never had to experience that.

I'd already fallen for Claire.

I'd already decided she was mine.

There was no going back.

* * *

Claire

I COULDN'T STOP THINKING ABOUT him. Just the thought of Xavier had chills racing up my arm and legs. I wrapped the blanket around me tighter and stared at the fire. I was in an office, or maybe it was a library. There was a desk off to the side and built-in bookshelves all around me. The fireplace was lit, the flames dancing over the logs as if they were alive and trying to seduce them.

I thought about him watching me earlier today, how I'd felt. Xavier was a big, strong man, but he kept to himself. He didn't speak much, but I could see that he was always taking in his surroundings. I thought about the way he made me feel, how just a look from him could light my body on fire. Even now I was aroused, so wet between my legs I was growing uncomfortable.

I heard something behind me and glanced over my shoulder at the door. It was slightly open, and I could see the man who consumed my thoughts standing there watching me. He had this expression on his face I couldn't really place. The way he looked at me made me feel like he wanted to know more. Or maybe I just wanted him to want to know more about me.

"May I join you?"

I found myself nodding instantly. He stepped into the room and made his way toward me, sitting in the chair across from me.

I was on the floor in front of the fire, the blanket wrapped around me, my legs curled up under my bottom. For long moments we just sat there, neither speaking but the air comfortable, the atmosphere almost relaxing.

"How are you liking it here?"

I glanced over at him, thinking about his question. Then I stared back at the flames for a prolonged moment.

"I've never felt safer," I admitted honestly. I looked back at him, but he showed no reaction, no emotion. He finally nodded and looked at the fire, maybe thinking about what I'd just said.

"You never have to worry about that again." He looked at me then. "You never have to worry about someone taking you. You don't ever have to fear stepping outside." His voice was growing lower, deeper, and I could see he was getting angry. "I'm going to make sure that you're always safe, Claire. You mean a lot to me."

That last part had my heart beating fast.

"I mean a lot to you?" I pursed my lips and cursed myself for speaking the words.

When he looked at me, I felt like he could see into my soul. "Claire, you mean more to me than any other woman ever has." My throat tightened at his words. "I've made it my life's mission to help women off the auction block. Never once have I wanted them, wanted to keep them." He leaned forward, his forearms braced on his knees. He was looking directly into my eyes now. "But then you came along and something in me changed, shifted."

"Shifted how?" My voice was so low, barely a whisper.

"Shifted in the way where I don't want to set you free." There was a hint of desperation in his voice. But the way he was looking at me was how I imagined a predator looks at his prey. "It's in the way that I want you as mine." His expression was so serious in this moment. "Does that frighten you?"

I didn't know what to say or how to feel. Emotions were swirling inside of me, threatening to take me under. "No," I answered honestly. In fact, it made me aroused to hear him say those things. I'd never admit that to him, couldn't because I was too shy, but I had no doubts that he could see how I felt in the way I held myself. He had to be able to read people because of what he did, how he lived his life.

Before I could say anything, he was standing. I straightened, not sure if he was leaving, but a part of me wanted to beg him to stay. I liked his company, liked having him here with me even if we didn't speak. "You're going?" I cleared my throat, wondering if I sounded desperate.

He smiled at me, and I swear something in me lit up. "I have some work to do, unfortunately, even if I'd like to stay here with you. But we'll talk more." He held his hand out, and I found myself slipping my fingers on top of his. He helped me to stand, and I wondered if he was going to pull me in for an embrace. Instead he reached out and tucked a stray piece of hair behind my ear.

He looked into my eyes but didn't speak, and neither did I. I didn't know what to say after what he'd told me. I wanted to admit that I desired him, too. I wanted to let him know that I didn't want to leave, that I didn't want to be set free. Being here had opened up my eyes, made me feel things I never thought I'd be able to experience. It was all so crazy and so fast. But it felt genuine. I always went with my gut instincts; I'd had to if I wanted to survive.

And being here with Xavier felt right. It felt as though this was where I belonged.

Claimed is Available Now

VICTORIA ASHLEY

VICTORIA ASHLEY GREW UP IN Rockford, IL and has had a passion for reading for as long as she can remember. After finding a reading app where it allowed readers to upload their own stories, she gave it a shot and writing became her passion.

She lives for a good romance book with tattooed bad boys that are just highly misunderstood and is not afraid to be caught crying during a good read. When she's not reading or writing about bad boys, you can find her watching her favorite shows such as Supernatural, Sons Of Anarchy and The Walking Dead.

Contact her at:
www.victoriaashleyauthor.com
www.facebook.com/VictoriaAshleyAuthor
Twitter: @VictoriaAauthor
Intstagram: VictoriaAshley.Author

BOOKS BY VICTORIA ASHLEY

WALK OF SHAME SERIES
Slade (Book 1)
Hemy (Book 2)
Cale (Book 3)

WALK OF SHAME 2ND GENERATION SERIES
Stone (Book 1)
Styx (Book 2)
Kash (Book 3)

SAVAGE & INK SERIES
Royal Savage (Book 1)
Beautiful Savage (Book 2) ~ Coming Soon

THE PAIN SERIES
Get Off On the Pain (Book 1)
Something For the Pain (Book 2)

STAND ALONE TITLES
Wake Up Call
This Regret
Thrust
Hard & Reckless
Strung

BOOKS CO-WRITTEN WITH JENIKA SNOW
LOCKE BROTHERS SERIES
Damaged Locke (Book 1)
Savage Locke (Book 2)
Twisted Locke (Book 3)

BOOKS CO-WRITTEN WITH HILARY STORM
ALPHACHAT.COM SERIES
Pay For Play (Book 1)
Two Can Play (Book 2)

JENIKA SNOW

JENIKA SNOW IS A USA Today bestselling Author of romance. She's a mother, wife, and nurse, and has been published since 2009. When not writing she can be found enjoying gloomy, rain-filled days, and wearing socks year-round.

Contact her at:
www.JenikaSnow.com
www.facebook.com/jenikasnow
Twitter: @jenikasnow
Intstagram: @jenikasnow

You can find more information on all her titles at:
www.JenikaSnow.com

ACKNOWLEDGMENTS

VICTORIA ASHLEY

FIRST AND FOREMOST, I'D LIKE to say a HUGE thank you to Jenika Snow for taking a chance and writing this amazing story with me.

I'd also like to thank the beta readers that took the time to read Twisted Locke. We appreciate you ladies so much!

And I want to say a big thank you to all of my loyal readers that have given me support over the last couple of years and have encouraged me to continue with my writing. Your words have all inspired me to do what I enjoy and love. Each and every one of you mean a lot to me and I wouldn't be where I am if it weren't for your support and kind words.

Last but not least, I'd like to thank all of the wonderful book bloggers that have taken the time to support our book and help spread the word. You all do so much for us authors and it is greatly appreciated. I have met so many friends on the way and you guys are never forgotten. You guys rock. Thank you!

JENIKA SNOW

A BIG THANK YOU TO Victoria for going on this adventure with me and creating dark and twisted characters that we love to hate! This story wouldn't be possible without help from so many people: Dana, our cover designer, Lindsey, who took the time to go over the story and give us her opinion, Kasi Alexander, who is an incredible editor, and of course all the readers and bloggers who support our crazy endeavors.

Made in the USA
Las Vegas, NV
24 July 2021